PENGUIN BOOKS

HECTOR AND THE SECRETS OF LOVE

François Lelord has had a successful career as a psychiatrist in France, where he was born, and in the United States, where he did his postdoc (UCLA). He is the co-author of a number of bestselling self-help books and has consulted for companies interested in reducing stress for their employees. He was on a trip to Hong Kong, questioning his personal and professional life, when the Hector character popped into his mind, and he wrote *Hector and the Search for Happiness*, the first novel in the series, not quite knowing what kind of book he was writing. The huge success of *Hector*, first in France, then in Germany and other countries, led him to spend more time writing and traveling, and at the height of the SARS epidemic he found himself in Vietnam, where he practiced psychiatry for a French NGO whose profits go toward heart surgery for poor Vietnamese children. While in Vietnam he also met his future wife, Phuong; today they live in Thailand.

François Lelord's series of novels about Hector's journeys includes *Hector and the Search for Happiness* and *Hector and the Search for Lost Time*. Turn to the back of this book for the opening chapters of *Hector and the Search for Lost Time*.

Hector and the Secrets of Love

A Novel

François Lelord

PENGUIN BOOKS

To all those who have been the inspiration for Hector

PENGUIN BOOKS
Published by the Penguin Group
Penguin Group (USA) Inc., 375 Hudson Street, New York, New York 10014, U.S.A.
Penguin Group (Canada), 90 Eglinton Avenue East, Suite 700, Toronto, Ontario, Canada M4P 2Y3 (a division of Pearson Penguin Canada Inc.) • Penguin Books Ltd, 80 Strand, London WC2R 0RL, England • Penguin Ireland, 25 St Stephen's Green, Dublin 2, Ireland (a division of Penguin Books Ltd) • Penguin Group (Australia), 250 Camberwell Road, Camberwell, Victoria 3124, Australia (a division of Pearson Australia Group Pty Ltd) • Penguin Books India Pvt Ltd, 11 Community Centre, Panchsheel Park, New Delhi–110 017, India • Penguin Group (NZ), 67 Apollo Drive, Rosedale, Auckland 0632, New Zealand (a division of Pearson New Zealand Ltd) • Penguin Books (South Africa) (Pty) Ltd, 24 Sturdee Avenue, Rosebank, Johannesburg 2196, South Africa

Penguin Books Ltd, Registered Offices: 80 Strand, London WC2R 0RL, England

First published in Great Britain by Gallic Books 2011
Published in Penguin Books 2011

1 3 5 7 9 10 8 6 4 2

Translation by Lorenza Garcia

Originally published in French as *Hector et les secrets de l'amour* by Éditions Odile Jacob, Paris.

Page 282 constitutes an extension of this copyright page.

LIBRARY OF CONGRESS CATALOGING IN PUBLICATION DATA
Lelord, François.
[Hector et les secrets de l'amour. English]
Hector and the secrets of love : a novel / François Lelord.
p. cm.
ISBN 978-0-14-311947-0
1. Psychiatrists—Fiction. 2. Love—Philosophy—Fiction. I. Title.
PQ2672.E489H4313 2011
843.92—dc22 2011007039

Printed in the United States of America

Contents

'ALL we have to say to him is: "My dear doctor, you're going to help us discover the secret of love." I'm sure he'll consider it a very noble mission.'

'Do you think he's up to it?'

'Yes, I do.'

'He'll need persuading – you have the necessary funds.'

'The most important thing, I think, is to make him feel he'll be doing something worthwhile.'

'So we'll need to tell him everything?'

'Yes. Well, not everything, if you see what I mean.'

'I understand.'

The two men in grey suits were talking late at night in a big office at the top of a tall building. Through the picture windows the bright city lights shone as far as the eye could see, but they didn't take any notice of them.

Instead they looked at some photographs they had taken from a file. They were glossy portraits of a youngish man with a preoccupied air.

'Psychiatrist, what a strange occupation!' said the older man. 'I wonder how anyone can stand it.'

'Yes, I wonder, too.'

The younger man, a tall, strapping fellow with cold eyes, replaced all the photos in the file, which was marked 'Dr Hector'.

HECTOR AND THE CHINESE PICTURE

ONCE upon a time there was a young psychiatrist called Hector.

Psychiatry is an interesting profession, but it can be very difficult, and quite tiring as well. In order to make it less tiring, Hector had brightened up his consulting room with some of his favourite pictures. In particular, a picture he'd brought back from China. It was a large redwood panel decorated with beautiful Chinese characters – or, for those who like to call things by their proper names, ideograms. When Hector felt tired after listening to all the problems people talked to him about, he would look at the beautiful gilded Chinese script carved in the wood and feel better. The people sitting in the chair opposite him talking about their problems would sometimes glance at the Chinese panel. It often seemed to Hector that it had a calming effect on his patients.

A few of them would ask Hector what the Chinese characters meant, and this embarrassed Hector because he didn't know. He couldn't read Chinese, still less speak it (even though he'd once met a nice Chinese girl, over in China). When you're a doctor, it's never very good to let your patients see that there's something you're not sure about, because they like to think that you know everything; it reassures them. And so Hector would invent a different saying each time, trying to come up with the one he thought would do most good to the person concerned.

For example, to Sophie, a woman who had got divorced the previous year and was still very angry with the father of her children, Hector explained that the expression in Chinese meant 'He who spends too long regretting his ruined crop will neglect to plant next year's harvest'.

Sophie had opened her eyes wide and after that she'd almost stopped talking to Hector about what a dreadful man her ex-husband was.

To Roger, a man who had a habit of talking to God in a very loud voice in the street (he believed God talked to him, too, and could even hear his words echoing in his head), Hector said that the expression meant 'The wise man is silent when communing with God'.

Roger replied that this was all very well for the god of the Chinese people, but that he, Roger, was talking to the real God, and so it was only natural for him to speak loud and clear. Hector agreed, but added that, since God could hear and understand everything, there was no need for Roger to talk to Him out loud; it was enough just to think of Him. Hector was trying to save Roger from getting into trouble when he was out and about, and from being put in hospital for long periods. Roger said that he ended up in hospital so often because it was the will of God, and that suffering was a test of faith.

On the one hand, Hector felt that the new treatment he'd prescribed Roger had helped him express himself more clearly and made him a lot more talkative, but, on the other, it didn't make Hector's job any less tiring.

Actually what Hector found most tiring was the question of love. Not in his own life, but in the lives of all the people who came to see him.

Because love, it seemed, was an endless source of suffering.

Some people complained of not having any at all.

'Doctor, I'm bored with my life; I feel so unhappy. I'd really like to be in love, to feel loved. It seems as if love is only for other people, not for me.'

This was the sort of thing Anne-Marie would say, for example. When she had asked Hector what the Chinese expression meant, Hector had looked at her very carefully. Anne-Marie could have been pretty if only she'd stopped dressing like her mother and hadn't focused all her energy on her work. Hector replied, 'If you want to catch fish, you must go to the river.'

Soon afterwards, Anne-Marie joined a choir. She started wearing make-up and stopped dressing like her mother all the time.

Some people complained of too much love. Too much love was as bad for their health as too much cholesterol.

'It's terrible – I should stop; I know that it's over, but I can't help thinking about him all the time. Do you think I should write to him . . . or call him? Or should I wait outside his office to try to see him?'

This was Claire, who, as can often happen, had become involved with a man who wasn't free, and to begin with it was fun because, as she told Hector, she wasn't in love, but then she did fall in love, and so did he. Even so, they decided to stop seeing each other because the man's wife was becoming suspicious and he didn't want to leave her. And so Claire suffered a lot, and when she asked Hector what the words on the Chinese panel said, he had to think for a moment before coming up with a reply: 'Do not build your home in a neighbour's field'.

Claire had burst into tears and Hector hadn't felt very pleased with himself.

He also saw men who suffered because of love, and these cases were even more serious: men only find the courage to go to a psychiatrist when they're very, very unhappy or when they've exhausted all their friends with their problems and have begun drinking too much.

This was the case with Luc – a boy who was a bit too nice and suffered a lot when women left him, especially as he often chose women who were not very nice, probably because his mother hadn't been very nice to him when he was little. Hector told him that the Chinese panel said: 'If you are scared of the panther, hunt the antelope'. And then he wondered whether there were any antelopes in China. Luc replied, 'That's a rather bloodthirsty proverb. The Chinese are quite bloodthirsty, aren't they?'

Hector realised that it wasn't going to be easy.

Some people, very many actually, both men and women, complained that they used to be madly in love with someone (usually someone they were living with) but that they no longer felt the same way, even though they were still very fond of them.

'I tell myself that maybe it's natural after all these years. We still get on very well, but we haven't made love for months . . . Together, I mean.'

For these people, Hector had a bit of trouble finding a suitable meaning for the Chinese panel, or else he'd come up with clichéd expressions like 'The wise man sees the beauty of each season', which meant nothing, even to him.

Some people complained of being in love, but with the wrong person.

'Oh dear, I know he'll end up being a disaster just like all the others. But I can't help myself.'

This was Virginie. She went from love affair to love affair with men who were very attractive to women, which was very exciting to begin with, but rather painful in the end. For her, Hector came up with: 'He who hunts must start again each day, while he who cultivates can watch his rice growing'.

Virginie said it was amazing how much the Chinese managed to say in just four characters, and Hector felt she was perhaps a little bit cleverer than him.

Other people had found love, but worried about it even so.

'We love each other, of course. But is he the right person for me? Marriage isn't to be taken lightly. When you marry, it's for life. And, anyway, I want to enjoy my freedom a bit longer . . . '

Hector generally asked these people to tell him about their mothers and fathers and how they got along.

Other people wondered whether they could ever hope to find love, whether perhaps it wasn't too good for them.

'I can't imagine anybody finding me attractive. Deep down, I don't think I'm a very interesting person. Even you seem bored, Doctor.'

At this point Hector woke up completely and said, no, not at all, and then kicked himself because the right thing to say would have been: 'What makes you think that?'

So a lot of people came to explain to Hector that love or lack of love prevented them from sleeping, thinking, laughing and in some cases even from living. And with this last category Hector had to be very careful, because he knew that love can make people kill themselves, which is a very foolish thing to do, so don't ever do it and if you have thoughts about doing it go to see someone like Hector immediately, or call a close friend.

Hector had been in love, and he remembered how much suffering love can cause: days and nights spent thinking about somebody who doesn't want to see you any more, wondering whether it would be better to write, to call or to remain in silence, unable to sleep unless you drink everything in the mini-bar of the hotel room in the town you've come to in order to see her except that she doesn't want to see you. Now, of course, this type of memory helped him to understand people who found themselves in the same situation. Hector also remembered the nice girls whom he had made suffer because of love and he wasn't very proud of that. They had loved him and he had only liked them. Sometimes, he'd lived through both roles, victim and executioner, with the same girl, because love is complicated, and, what's worse, it's unpredictable.

This type of suffering was now a thing of the past for Hector. (Or so he thought at the beginning of this story, but just wait and see.) Because he had a good friend, Clara, whom he loved very much and she loved him, and they were even thinking of having a baby together and of getting married. Hector was happy because in the end love affairs are very tiring, so when you find somebody you love and who loves you, you really hope that it will be your last love affair.

The strange thing is that, at the same time, you wonder if it isn't a bit sad to think that it will be your last love affair. You see how complicated love is!

HECTOR LOVES CLARA

ONE evening Hector arrived home, preoccupied with all the painful stories about love he'd heard during the day: situations in which one person loved more than the other, or both people loved each other but they didn't get on, or they no longer loved each other but couldn't love anybody else, and other permutations besides, because whereas happiness in love offers a beautiful, relatively unchanging landscape, unhappiness comes in many and varied forms, as a great Russian author once put it slightly better.

Clara wasn't home yet, because she always had meetings that finished late. She worked for a big pharmaceutical company, which produced many best-selling drugs. The big company enjoyed swallowing up smaller companies, and one day it even tried to devour a company larger than itself, but the larger company fought it off.

Clara's bosses were pleased with her because she was a very conscientious, hard-working girl, and they often asked her to stand in for them at meetings or sum up long reports for them, which they didn't have time to read.

Hector was happy to know that Clara's bosses had faith in her. On the other hand he didn't like her coming home so late, often tired, and not always in a very good mood. Because, although her bosses depended on her a lot, they never took her along to the really important meetings with the real big shots; they went to those on their own, and made out that they were the ones who had done all the work or come up with all the good ideas.

What a surprise, then, when Clara arrived home with a big smile on her face.

'Good day?' asked Hector, pleased to see Clara looking so happy.

'Oh, not great, too many meetings getting in the way of work. And everybody is in a panic because the patent on our leading drug has expired. So we can kiss our profits goodbye!'

'But you look so happy.'

'I'm happy to see you, my love.'

And she began to laugh. You see, this was Clara's way of jesting about love. Luckily, Hector was used to it and he knew that Clara really loved him.

'Well,' said Clara, 'it's true, but I'm also happy because we've received an invitation.'

'We?'

'Yes, well, you're the one invited, but I'm allowed to go with you.' Clara took a letter out of her briefcase and gave it to Hector. 'They should really have posted it to you, but they're aware by now that we know each other.'

Hector read the letter. It was written by a man who was very high up in Clara's company, one of the real big shots she didn't meet very often. He said that he thought very highly of Hector (Hector remembered they'd shaken hands twice at conferences on psychiatry) and was relying on him to take part in a confidential meeting, where people from the company would ask his opinion on a very important matter. He hoped that Hector would agree to go, and repeated how much he appreciated his expertise.

Together with the letter was another piece of paper showing the place where the meeting would be held: a very pretty hotel made of wood overlooking a magnificent beach with palm trees. The hotel was on a faraway island surrounded by a very blue sea. Hector wondered why they had to take them so far. It was perfectly possible to think at home in an armchair, but he told himself that this was the company's way of making him feel that he was important to them.

There was a third piece of paper telling Hector that in addition to the invitation he would of course be paid for giving his opinion. When he saw the amount, he thought he'd misread it and had added on an extra zero, but on rereading it he realised that he hadn't, that it was right.

'Hasn't there been some mistake?' Hector asked Clara.

'No, that's the correct amount. The others are getting the same – more or less what they asked for.'

'The others?'

She gave Hector the names of his fellow psychiatrists who had also been invited.

Hector knew them. There was a very old psychiatrist with a bow tie who, as he grew older, had specialised in rich unhappy people (though he also occasionally saw poor people and didn't charge them), and a jolly little woman who had specialised in people who had difficulty doing what people in love do, and were willing to pay crazy amounts of money in order to be able to do it.

'Right, well, this will be a mini holiday for us,' said Hector.

'Speak for yourself,' said Clara. 'I'll be seeing the same old faces I see at every meeting.'

'At least we'll be going away somewhere together for a change,' said Hector.

'We went to Italy recently!'

'That was only because you had a conference there afterwards. Your job always determines everything.'

'Would you prefer me to be a good little housewife and stay at home?'

'No, I'd prefer you to stop letting yourself be exploited, and come home at a reasonable time.'

'I bring you a piece of good news and you immediately start complaining!'

'You're the one who started it.'

'No, I didn't, you did.'

Hector and Clara carried on bickering and went to bed without speaking to each other or kissing each other good night. Which just goes to show that love isn't easy, even for psychiatrists.

During the night, Hector woke up. In the dark, he found his luminous pen, which allowed him to write at night without waking Clara up. He noted: *Perfect love would be never having arguments.*

He thought about it. He wasn't sure.

He didn't feel he could call his statement a 'lesson'. Wanting to give lessons on love seemed a bit ridiculous. He thought of 'reflection', but it was too serious for such a simple phrase. It was only a tiny thought, like a seedling that has just sprouted and nobody knows what it will be yet. There, he'd found it. It was a seedling. He wrote:

Seedling no. 1: Perfect love would be never having arguments.

He thought for a little bit longer, but it was difficult as his eyelids kept closing. He looked at Clara who was sleeping.

Seedling no. 2: Sometimes we argue most with the people we love the most.

HECTOR AND CLARA GO TO THE BEACH

One place on the island's beach seemed to belong to a large family of little pink crabs that were constantly mounting or fighting each other. Hector watched them, and he very quickly understood that when they mounted each other it was the males mounting the females and when they fought it was the males fighting amongst themselves. And why were they fighting? To be able to mount the females, of course. Even for crabs, love seemed like quite a difficult thing, especially for the males that lost a pincer during a fight. It reminded Hector of something one of his patients had said to him about a woman he was very much in love with: 'I would have done better to cut my arm off than meet her.' He was exaggerating of course, especially as, unlike with crabs, an arm doesn't grow back.

'You like your little friends the crabs, don't you?'

It was Clara, who had arrived wearing a pretty white bathing suit. She had started to tan a little and to Hector she looked as appetising as a freshly picked apricot.

'You're crazy, be careful, people can see us! And so can the crabs!'

Exactly! It was watching the crabs that had given Hector ideas, but he had also just noticed that the people from the company were looking in their direction. They were having a drink on the veranda of the hotel's biggest bungalow, which was built on stilts. The sunset was magnificent, the waves breaking on the beach made a gentle murmur, Clara looked all golden in the setting sun and Hector thought: This is a moment of happiness. He had learnt that you mustn't waste any of these.

It gets dark very quickly in that part of the world, and everybody met for dinner in the big bungalow. And what was for starters? Crab!

'We're delighted you could all be here,' said the very important man from the company, whose name was Gunther. He had a slight accent and broad shoulders. He was very tall, but came from a very small, very rich country specialising in chocolate bars and big pharmaceutical companies.

'Yes, indeed!' said his colleague, Marie-Claire, a tall redhead with a dazzling smile and magnificent sparkling rings.

Hector had noticed she and Clara didn't like each other very much.

The old psychiatrist who had been invited didn't respond; he was concentrating on his crab. He wasn't wearing his bow tie and the strange thing was that in a polo shirt he looked even older. There's a good piece of advice, thought Hector. When you get very old, always wear a bow tie. He began thinking about what to advise very old ladies. To wear a hat?

'I've been here before,' said Ethel, the woman who was an expert in love, 'and I adored it.'

And she mentioned the name of another big pharmaceutical company that had invited her to that same island, and Hector saw a touch of annoyance in Gunther's and Marie-Claire's smiles.

But Ethel didn't notice a thing. As previously mentioned, she was a jolly little woman who was always cheerful, which must have done the people who went to see her a lot of good.

'Did you know the redness in crabs is sexual?' she asked. 'In proportion to their size, they are extremely well endowed!'

And she gave her jolly laugh again. Hector noticed that the maître d'hôtel, a tall, Asian-looking fellow, had been listening and had given a faint smile.

At either end of the table, there was a group of young men and women also employed by the company, and you could tell that some of the young men, and, of course, some of the young women, would one day be bosses.

And it was one of the girls who smiled at Hector and said to him, 'I really liked your last article. What you say is so true!'

This was an article Hector had written for a magazine explaining why so many people needed to see psychiatrists.

Hector said he was glad but, at the same time, he saw that Clara wasn't altogether happy about his little chat with the young woman.

Later, Clara whispered in his ear, 'She's always showing off, that girl.'

The old psychiatrist had finished shelling his crab, and he began delicately eating the tiny pile of meat he had collected in the middle of his plate.

'As methodical as ever, my dear,' Ethel said to him, chuckling. 'No pleasure without a struggle!'

The old psychiatrist replied without looking up from his plate, 'As you well know, my dear, at my age everything is a struggle, alas.'

And everybody laughed because he was the type of old-school psychiatrist who had a dry wit.

His name was François, and Hector liked him very much.

At the end of the meal, Gunther wished them all a very good night since tomorrow they were going to get up early for the meeting, and he added in Hector's language, 'The best advice is found on the pillow,' apparently very pleased at having learnt this expression because Hector's language was not Gunther's mother tongue; in the small country he came from they spoke several languages.

Much later, when Hector looked back on this whole affair and remembered 'The best advice is found on the pillow', he felt like laughing and crying at the same time.

HECTOR GOES TO A MEETING

'WELL,' said Gunther, 'we are all here this morning because we need to pick your brains. Our company is working on the drugs of the future. But we are well aware that we will only maintain our dominant position in the market if our drugs are really useful to patients, and who is better placed to know about patients than you?'

He talked a bit more about what wonderful people Hector, François – the old psychiatrist, and Ethel – the expert in love, were. Everybody had gathered, like at dinner the previous evening, in a big room made entirely of wood overlooking the beach.

Hector looked out of the huge glassless windows. The sea was grey that morning under a cloudy sky, giving the palm trees a melancholy air. He had realised the day before that if you went from the beach across the sea in a straight line, in a few days you would reach China. And, as previously mentioned, Hector had once met a pretty Chinese girl, and sometimes he still thought about her. But of course it was Clara he loved.

Actually, it was Clara who was talking now and projecting pretty pictures with a little computer.

'This shows the increase in the consumption of antidepressants in Western countries . . .'

People really did take a lot of them, more and more, and women twice as many as men.

'But, even so, half of all depressive illnesses still go undiagnosed and untreated,' Clara went on.

It was true; Hector sometimes saw people who had suffered from depression for years without ever receiving treatment. On the other hand, a lot of people took antidepressants without really needing them. But of course the pharmaceutical company was less concerned about that.

As he watched Clara, who was such a good speaker, so confident and so elegant in her white linen suit, Hector felt quite proud that a girl like her had chosen him out of all the men who chased after her. When he remembered all the effort he had put into it at the time, and the crabs fighting on the beach, he resolved to write in his notebook:

Seedling no. 3: You cannot win someone's love without a fight.

Clara talked about the new antidepressant the company would soon launch onto the market, which would be more effective and better tolerated than all the others. With this one even the most depressed people would be singing and dancing in the street.

Gunther thanked Clara for her 'brilliant contribution' and Hector noticed this upset Marie-Claire, the tall redhead, a little bit. But, well, that's the way it always is in companies.

'We have talked about antidepressants,' said Gunther, 'to give you an idea of how we see the future. But, in reality, depression will soon be a thing of the past, from our point of view, in any case. It will soon be just a question of monitoring people.'

The phrase 'monitoring people' sent a slight shiver down Hector's spine, although Gunther wasn't wrong.

'. . . but depression is an illness,' Gunther went on, 'and people today don't just want their illnesses cured, they want to be healthy, meaning they want to enjoy "physical and mental well-being". Those aren't my words – they come from the World Health Organization. In short, people want to be ha-ppy!'

And Gunther let out a big booming laugh that showed off his splendid teeth. All the young people smiled.

From time to time, the tall maître d'hôtel from the evening before and a young waitress in a sarong came in to serve them coffee, and Hector said to himself that they probably weren't worried about being 'ha-ppy', but about feeding their families. He knew that the price of a room for one night in that hotel was equivalent to two months' average wages in the country to which the island belonged and, at the same time, this provided jobs for a lot of people who could then support their whole family.

He also noticed that every time the young girl came in, the old psychiatrist, François, followed her tenderly with his gaze. And when she left François looked a little sad. Hector thought that one day he would be like François, and that made him feel a little sad, too.

'They're right to want to be happy,' said Ethel. 'That's what life is all about!'

Ethel herself always looked happy – anyone would think she secreted the company's new antidepressant in her own brain. During the night, Hector had gone out onto the balcony for a breath of fresh air and had seen a tall figure coming out of Ethel's bungalow.

'Well,' said Gunther, 'I think we all agree with that evaluation of happiness. So, what is it in your opinion, besides illness, accidents and financial problems, that most stops people from being happy?'

There was a long silence. You could tell that everybody had ideas, but nobody dared to be the first to speak. Hector hesitated, because he wondered whether it was a good idea to bring up his idea without first having spoken to Clara about it, since this meeting was important to her and he had to consider her, too. But he had his own opinion about what stopped people from being happy.

'Love.'

Everybody looked at the old psychiatrist, François. It was he who had spoken. As previously mentioned, Hector liked him a lot.

HECTOR HEARS ABOUT LOVE

Old François looked out to sea as he spoke, as though the sight of it inspired him. And everybody listened in complete silence.

'Love,' he said, '*a sickness of the body to which the mind consents*. Not my words, unfortunately. Love certainly provides our greatest joys, although that word is inadequate; our greatest ecstasies, we might say. That movement towards the other, that moment when our dream becomes reality, that state of grace where at last we think of something other than ourselves, that meeting of bodies that makes us immortal, for a few moments at least, that transformation of the everyday in the presence of the loved one, ah . . . When their face is engraved on our heart, except that sometimes . . .' He sighed. 'Because love brings such suffering, oceans of suffering . . . spurned love, loving too much, a lack of love, the death of love, alas . . .

'What is left of our loving ways?
What is left of those sunny days . . .
Faded joys and windswept tresses
Stolen kisses and caresses
What is left of the love we knew?
Tell me now I beg of you . . .'

He finished the song, and Hector saw to his great surprise that Clara's eyes were glistening with tears. Old François suddenly noticed that everyone looked full of emotion, and he seemed to rouse himself.

'Forgive me, my friends, I got a little carried away; I just wanted to answer your question about what can make people unhappier.'

There was a brief silence. Gunther smiled and took the floor again. 'Thank you for your very remarkable rendition. Listening to you makes me feel as if I am truly hearing the language of love!'

In the meantime, the young girl in the sarong had returned, this time carrying a tray of fruit juice, and again old François followed her with forlorn eyes.

'And now,' Gunther went on, 'I turn to you, dear Ethel. I'd like to hear your opinion, which, I believe, is different.'

'Yes, it certainly is!' She turned to the old psychiatrist. 'My dear François, you painted a marvellous, if somewhat sad, portrait of love for us. But, after all, how dreary life would be without love! It is love that transports us, that fills us with joy! Love turns life into one long adventure, every encounter is a dazzling experience – well, not always, of course, but in actual fact, it is our less successful love affairs that enable us to appreciate the others. I think love protects us from one of the biggest problems facing the modern world: boredom. Because, well, the lives we lead are so safe – I mean in our countries, of course – that love is the only adventure we have left. Hurrah for love, which keeps us forever young!'

And, indeed, when you looked at Ethel, who was no longer exactly young but who had such a youthful air, you said to yourself that love certainly seemed to agree with her.

Gunther appeared delighted. 'Ah,' he said, 'what a joyous description of love you have given us, dear Ethel. And how joyful love is, to be sure! Speaking of which, if you'll allow me . . .'

Gunther rose to his full height and began singing in a fine bass voice.

'L is for the way you look at me
O is for the only one I see
V is very, very extraordinary
E is even more than anyone that you adore . . .
Love is all that I can give to you
Love is more than just a game for two . . .'

All the women round the table suddenly seemed mesmerised by Gunther's (very good) rendition of Nat King Cole. He had even acquired the self-assurance, easy smile and smouldering gaze of a real crooner, and Hector felt a pang of jealousy. He glanced at Clara but, amazingly, she seemed indifferent to Gunther's performance; in fact she looked a little annoyed, which made Hector love her all the more.

When he had finished, everybody applauded, even Hector, who regretted his pang of jealousy and who, with Clara's career in mind, didn't want to give a bad impression.

'Thank you, my friends,' said Gunther. 'I'm sorry, I still don't know any love poems in French, but next time you can depend on me! And now you, dear Dr Hector, what do you think about love?'

HECTOR TALKS ABOUT LOVE

Hector was embarrassed. He agreed with both François and Ethel. Depending on the day – and who he had listened to during the day – he could have sung an ode to love or, on the contrary, wished someone would hurry up and invent a vaccine against it. But in a meeting it isn't exactly impressive just to say you agree with what has already been said, because meetings are also occasions for showing off. And so Hector thought for a moment, and began.

'I think what both my colleagues have said about love is very true. Love is the source of our greatest joys and love is the cause of our deepest misfortunes.'

Hector noticed Clara was watching him, and was surprised to see she looked a little sad. Had François's song affected her to that extent? He went on.

'But, listening to my patients, I often say to myself that the main difficulty with love is that it is involuntary. We fall in love or stay in love with people who are unsuitable or who no longer love us and, conversely, we feel no love towards people who would be very suitable. Love is involuntary, that's the problem. Our personal histories prepare us to be attracted to people who unconsciously evoke emotions from our childhood or adolescence. I love you because unwittingly you provoke the same feelings in me as Mummy or Daddy, or my little brother or sister, or the opposite feelings, for that matter. And then there are the circumstances of our meeting. We all know that people fall in love more easily when they are already troubled by another emotion – surprise, or even fear or compassion' – an image flashed through his mind of tears streaming from pretty almond-shaped eyes, one evening in a taxi – 'because we know that any intense emotional state greatly increases the risk of falling in love. And we could also speak of the role music plays in the early stages of love, only I don't sing nearly as well as François, so I am not likely to move you to tears!'

They all laughed, which was good, because, although it wasn't obvious on the surface, François's speech had upset everyone a little.

'But I can recite a few verses,' Hector went on. 'Phaedra is about to marry Theseus; everything is wonderful until her future son-in-law Hippolytus, Theseus's son, turns up and disaster ensues!

'I blushed and went pale when first I saw him,
My mind was troubled, my eyes grew dim,
Love-struck I was unable to draw breath,
My body burned, I felt close to death.

'And, like poor Phaedra, we fall in love not with who we want to fall in love with, but with who moves us, and sometimes it is the last person we should fall in love with.

Our involuntary choice is not always the right one, and sometimes it is actually the worst one, hence our suffering. And then, of course, there is the completely different situation of the loving couple where, over the years, the love they once felt for each other fades and they can't go on. They feel their love dying, but are unable to bring it back to life.'

As he spoke, Hector noticed that Gunther and his colleague were watching him with special interest, which made him shudder, because he thought they looked a bit like cats sizing up a particularly appetising mouse. Suddenly he was certain these two had plans concerning him, and he wondered whether Clara knew.

HECTOR IS WORRIED

JUST after lunch, Hector and Clara went for a walk on the beach under the still cloudy sky.

'You looked sad just now,' said Hector.

'No, I wasn't sad,' said Clara. 'Or maybe I was, seeing your elderly colleague. I found what he said moving.'

'Yes, so did I.'

They had come to a small family of crabs. The struggle continued: fighting, mounting each other, fighting.

'We should show him these crabs. That would confirm his opinion: love, what misery!'

'Let's keep going,' Clara said, with a shudder.

They walked for a while in silence. Hector was worried; he sensed Clara wasn't her usual self.

'Is everything okay?' he asked.

'Yes, of course!'

Hector realised this wasn't the time to interrogate Clara, but he tried asking a different question.

'I had the feeling Gunther and Marie-Claire were looking at me in a funny way. As if they had something planned for me.'

Clara stopped and stared at him. She looked angry. 'And you think I wouldn't tell you if I knew?'

'That's not what I'm saying. I'm telling you what I felt.'

Clara pulled herself together. She thought it over then let out a sigh. 'It's possible. I was wondering the same thing.'

'Anyway, if I'm right, we'll soon find out. I'll try to be a credit to you.'

Clara smiled, but Hector thought he glimpsed traces of the sadness she had displayed earlier.

'Is everything okay?'

'Yes, yes. Oh, look, a weird crab.'

It was true: one crab was bigger than the others and was moving very slowly, pausing from time to time, as though observing the others scuffling around him. But he didn't try to fight, or mount any females. It looked as if he were watching, and then he moved off again with his slow, rather sad gait.

'It's your old colleague,' said Clara.

They both laughed because it was true, the old crab did look like François. Hector thought that life with Clara was wonderful for many reasons and one of them was because he and Clara laughed at the same things.

As a result, they began looking for Ethel among the other crabs, and they found her: a lively little female who kept scuttling from one crab to another.

Then Hector noticed a formidable-looking male with two huge pincers that the other crabs didn't even attempt to attack when he mounted a female.

'That's Gunther,' said Hector.

Clara smiled, but she still looked sad, Hector was sure of it. Suddenly he wondered whether he, too, wasn't about to become very unhappy because of love.

HECTOR ACCEPTS A MISSION

At the end of dinner, Gunther put down his cigar and leaned over to Hector. 'I'd like to have a quiet word with you,' he said.

'Whenever you like,' said Hector.

'We'll wait until the others have gone,' said Gunther.

Everyone seemed quite cheerful at dinner; they had the healthy glow of people who have been swimming in the sea and begun to get a tan, and even old François seemed very jaunty. He was chatting to a young employee of the company and making her laugh. Clara had begun a long discussion with Ethel, and Hector overheard the word 'multi-orgasmic', which Ethel seemed to repeat often.

And then everyone stood up and people began making their way back to their bungalows. Hector gave Clara a little wave, and she left, too. As he watched her walk through the door and glance back at him, Hector had another awful feeling, but he quickly told himself he was imagining things – he knew that Clara loved him.

The three of them, Hector, Gunther and Marie-Claire, sat facing one another in big armchairs made of tropical wood in the lounge area in Gunther's suite. Gunther relit his cigar and the tall maître d'hôtel came in with the drinks they had ordered: cognac for Gunther and Marie-Claire, and coconut milk with a straw for Hector, who had never liked drinking after dinner. The tall maître d'hôtel left the bottle of cognac next to Gunther.

It was dark outside, and you could hear the sound of the waves, and Hector thought about the crabs that were perhaps still making love under the moonlight.

A large file lay on the low table, and Hector was surprised to read on the cover the name of somebody he knew; it was the eminent professor of Happiness Studies he had met in the country of More, or, for people who are fond of geography, America. The eminent professor was a small, skinny man with a big nose and a big tuft of white hair, who spoke very quickly and who thought even more quickly. He was carrying out a lot of complicated research to try to discover whether happiness was largely a question of character (you are happy because you have a talent for happiness) or a question of circumstances (you are happy if you have things in your life that make you happy). The eminent professor's name was Cormorant, which was quite amusing because with his big nose and his tuft of white hair he looked a bit like the bird of the same name.

Hector liked him a lot and they often exchanged emails. Professor Cormorant told Hector things about happiness which gave him ideas about how to treat his unhappy patients. He and the professor very rarely met and there was a big age difference between them, but they had struck up a long-distance friendship.

'You know him,' said Gunther, taking a photo of Professor Cormorant from the file.

'Of course.'

'A brilliant mind.'

'Yes.'

'An outstanding researcher.'

'Without a doubt.'

Gunther took a puff of his cigar, as though to calm himself. Hector had the impression he was angry.

'He's working for us,' said Marie-Claire.

'On happiness?'

'No, on love.'

Marie-Claire explained that the big pharmaceutical company had funded some new research into love, and as Professor Cormorant was already a world expert in the study of emotions it had been easy for him to switch from happiness to love because both are combinations of complex emotions. Hector was very interested. The professor had never mentioned this new research to him.

'There was a confidentiality clause,' Marie-Claire explained, 'for him and his team of researchers. They were working in collaboration with our researchers.'

Hector looked out of the corner of his eye at Gunther, who was still puffing on his cigar as though to calm himself.

'Were you developing a new drug?'

'Do you remember what you were saying this morning? We don't choose who we fall in love with? We fall out of love with a person we'd like to go on loving? We're trying to find a solution to that problem.'

Hector was stunned. 'A drug for falling in love with whoever we want to? Or for staying in love when we want to?'

Marie-Claire didn't answer and looked at Gunther as though asking his permission to say more.

Gunther sighed.

'You've got it in one,' he said.

Hector began to think about all the effects a drug like that might have on people's lives. What if you gave it to someone without them knowing?

'We're in deep shit because of him,' said Gunther suddenly.

It was surprising to hear Gunther swear. This time Hector was sure Gunther was very angry with Professor Cormorant.

Gunther took a swig of cognac then gestured to Marie-Claire to carry on explaining the situation.

'Our research teams had developed three drugs that acted in three different ways. It was Professor Cormorant's job to study their effects on the love impulses of healthy volunteers. What we didn't know was that, aided by a chemist from his university, he had secretly modified the molecules of the drugs we had provided him with, which meant the psychological results he obtained related to those modified products, not to our original drugs.'

Hector said to himself he had always suspected the professor was a bit mad – now he knew for sure.

'And what were the results?'

'They were promising,' said Marie-Claire.

Hector sensed she wouldn't give any more away.

'We're in deep shit because of him,' Gunther repeated.

You could tell from his voice the cognac had begun to take effect.

Marie-Claire explained that one day the professor had wiped all the most recent results off the computers' hard disks and had disappeared with all the samples of the modified molecules.

'And the chemist?'

Again Marie-Claire looked at Gunther, who nodded.

'The chemist went mad.'

'Mad?'

'We think he tried to test one of the new drugs on himself. He's completely incoherent. He's been . . . committed.'

'That arsehole,' said Gunther, starting on his third cognac.

Marie-Claire went on to explain that this research into love had cost hundreds of millions of dollars and that they had been about to get some results when the professor had disappeared. Other rival companies were working on the same thing; it was like a multimillion-dollar race.

There was a silence. Seeing Gunther and Marie-Claire looking at him, a question occurred to Hector, the answer to which he was sure he already knew. He asked it just the same.

'And why are you telling me all this?'

'So you can find him,' said Gunther. 'We need to find Professor Cormorant.'

HECTOR TAKES TO THE AIR

Who are you to think you can tame love? Under the guise of relieving suffering you want to impose servitude. The control of feelings, that's your aim. Well, Professor Cormorant isn't going to help you. Professor Cormorant has a very different vision of the future that you cannot begin to imagine. All you can think about is stuffing people full of your little pills. Professor Cormorant pities you because he is a good man.

Professor Cormorant really had changed; he referred to himself in the third person in almost all the emails he had sent Gunther and Marie-Claire. An unexpected side effect of the new drugs he had taken with him perhaps?

Hector folded the letter and looked at the air hostess, who was bringing some champagne. This made him happy because he already knew the effect champagne had. In addition, the air hostess was wearing pretty oriental clothes, a dress with a slit up one side over silk trousers. And, you've guessed right, she was Asian, because Hector was on his way to a country very near China where they had most recently traced Professor Cormorant. Since that country had been occupied a long time ago by Hector's country, he was hoping to find a lot of people there who spoke his language, because Hector was not very good at languages, and Asian languages aren't the easiest ones to speak, let alone write.

But the air hostess only spoke English. She asked Hector if he was visiting her country as a tourist or on business and Hector said 'tourist', and wondered how the young woman would have responded if he had told her he was going in search of a mad professor.

Talking a little to the air hostess and drinking champagne did Hector good; it stopped him from thinking about Clara.

Before leaving on this mission, he and Clara had had a long talk. Or rather he had started off asking Clara a lot of questions to find out why she often looked sad. At first she had said no, it was nothing, she wasn't sad, Hector was imagining things, and then she had finally told him she still loved him, but she wondered whether she was really *in* love with him. Hector hadn't taken it too badly, because when you are a psychiatrist you are used to remaining calm while you listen to what people say, and people say very strange things sometimes, but even so, there on the plane he needed to drink champagne and talk to the air hostess in order to repress the urge to pick up the telephone fitted to his seat and call Clara at half-hourly intervals. Especially because he knew it wouldn't have done much good and he would quickly have run up a phone bill that would have shocked even Gunther.

Love is universal – saying this might make us wonder whether we have made any progress at all, but of course we have, because it allows us to jettison all those silly cultural prejudices, hey presto. Regardless of race, culture or the regime imposed on us, love sets us all aquiver. Just take a look at all the world's love poems throughout the ages and I guarantee you will find in them universal themes: the sorrow of being parted from the loved one, the joy of seeing him or her again, odes to his or her beauty and the promise of ecstasy it brings, the desire to see him or her triumph or escape from danger. Do it and you will see I am right and that will shut you up, you dimwits.

Before writing this message, it would seem Professor Cormorant had taken another type of pill. Hector had quivered slightly when he read *the sorrow of being parted from the loved one*, but he managed to focus again in order to read all the professor's most recent emails since he had gone missing. There were about fifty of them and Hector thought that by examining them he might discover what was going on in the professor's mind, understand what he wanted, and eventually find him.

Others at the company had tried this of course, but without any success; in their view, Professor Cormorant had gone mad, and that was that.

The only thing they could do was find out where the emails had been sent from, and this was very clever of them, because the professor had done some quite complicated things to prevent them from discovering which computer he had used. As a result, it took the people from the company several days to locate the computer and by the time they sent somebody there the professor had gone.

Hector had a map of the world recording the professor's movements.

It was evident that all the most recent emails had been sent from Asia, so there was a chance they would find him there. But what Gunther was counting on most was the professor wanting to talk to Hector. Before leaving, Hector had sent the professor an email.

Dear Professor Cormorant,

Some people you know well want to find you. They are sending me after you in the hope that I will have a better chance of finding you than they do. It would give me great pleasure to talk to you anyway and to hear how you are getting on. You may reply to me at this address, which only I have access to.

Yours sincerely

Hector didn't really know what he would do if he found Professor Cormorant. Of course, he was being paid by Gunther to find him and bring him back, but, as you have already guessed, Hector liked the professor more than he liked Gunther, and also he said to himself that the professor might have had very good reasons for disappearing.

The air hostess brought him more champagne with a smile, and Hector felt a sudden flash of love for her. Perhaps he could ask her for her number?

He told himself he was pathetic.

He opened his little notebook and wrote:

Seedling no. 4: True love is not wanting to be unfaithful.

He looked at the air hostess walking away in her pretty oriental outfit then he mused some more and wrote:

Seedling no. 5: True love is not being unfaithful (even when you want to be).

HECTOR DOES SOME HISTORY AND GEOGRAPHY

After taking another plane, this time one with propellers that juddered quite a lot, Hector arrived in a small town in the middle of the jungle. The town centre had been built a long time ago by people from his country and it looked just like a sleepy town from his childhood, with its post office and town hall, a canal lined with tall trees, and the Café des Amis. But, of course, the people who lived here were Asians who strolled in a leisurely manner and drank at the Café des Amis and other bars, particularly the men, because in this country, like many others, it was mostly the women who did the work. As soon as you went a little way from the centre, the roads were no longer tarmacked, except in the hotel district where they widened out again and were lined with palm trees. Because in this country they had built a lot of hotels in huge gardens full of marvellous trees. Beautiful hotels made half out of wood with roofs that blended in with the local architecture and balconies on stilts, because they had been built not very long ago, after the period when architects were crazy and planted huge cement blocks all over the world.

The architects who certainly weren't crazy were the ones who, a few centuries earlier, had conceived the huge stone temples you found in the forests near the town, at around the same time that people in Hector's country were building cathedrals. There were dozens of temples scattered over several miles and people came from all over the world to see them. It was the architects of those temples, then, who had provided work for their colleagues who had built the hotels centuries later, and who should perhaps have raised another little temple to their predecessors.

The manager of one of the town's most delightful hotels was quite young and cheerful; he wore a shirt with button-down pockets and looked a bit like Tintin. He clearly remembered the professor who often sent emails from the business centre at his hotel.

'He left three days ago. He told me he was going to Laos. Why are you looking for him?'

'He's a friend of mine,' said Hector. 'My other friends and I have been a bit worried about him lately.'

'Ah,' said the hotel manager.

He nodded without saying anything and Hector could see that several thoughts were flashing through his mind. Hector understood at once: hotel managers are a bit like psychiatrists: they see and hear many things they mustn't tell anybody. It's called professional confidentiality. Hector had always got on well with hotel managers – to start with because he liked hotels and it is always better when you know the manager, but also because, with all their guests and staff, hotel managers end up learning a thing or two about human nature, a bit like psychiatrists, but they're often cleverer.

Hector knew how to put the hotel manager at his ease (we won't tell you how because psychiatrists have to keep some things to themselves, a bit like magicians) and the manager began to talk about Professor Cormorant.

'At first, we found him charming. Also, he picked up a few words in Khmer quite quickly and everybody was impressed. The staff adored him. He always had a kind word for everyone. He visited the temples in the late afternoon when the crowds of tourists have left and the light is at its most beautiful. And he spent a lot of time working in his room. One evening, I invited him to dinner.'

The professor had explained to the hotel manager that he was an expert in butterflies and was in search of a very rare species which all the other experts thought was extinct, but he was convinced a few specimens still survived in the area surrounding one of the temples deep in the jungle.

'I tried to dissuade him from going there because that temple is in a region that isn't safe, and there are still a lot of landmines around it.'

What we haven't told you is that this beautiful country had a terrible history: crazy leaders who had studied abstract reasoning during their time in Hector's country had decided to come back and purge their country. And, be warned, the moment a great leader mentions the word 'purge' you know how it will end – that's to say very badly. Almost a third of the country's population was exterminated in the name of Good. Since his arrival, Hector had only met smiling young men and smiling young women, but he had the feeling that these smiles concealed terrible stories of childhoods without parents or with parents who had been forced into becoming executioners or victims or both. And there were a lot of landmines left over from that period, which occasionally exploded underneath fathers tilling their fields or children playing at the side of a road cleared of mines.

'And he still went to visit the temple?'

'Well, that's what he told me, at any rate. The problems started when he got back.'

The hotel manager explained that the professor had begun pestering the masseuses.

'The masseuses?'

'Yes, we offer our guests traditional massages. But strictly massages, if you see what I mean, nothing more. If people want something different, there are places for that in town, but we cater to families with children here, and the two things don't mix. Anyway, he became very persistent with the masseuses and they came and told me. I then had a word with him, which is always a little embarrassing, but clients who come on strong with the staff is one of the situations you have to deal with in a hotel, especially here, you understand.'

Hector had glimpsed some of the young female staff in the lobby, and he understood.

'And how did he take it?'

'Very oddly. He laughed, as if I were joking, only I wasn't joking at all. Anyway, I assumed he'd understood and was laughing to save face, the way people here often do, in fact.'

'And had he understood?'

'I don't think so. The next day, he left. With one of our masseuses.'

HECTOR MEETS VAYLA

Hector wanted to meet one of the friends of the masseuse who had run away with Professor Cormorant. The hotel manager agreed and told him that the masseuse was very good friends with a young waitress she had helped to get a job here, because they came from the same village. And so Hector found himself in an office with a shy young girl in a sarong, who gave him a charming oriental greeting, bringing her hands together and bowing her head, and another young woman from reception who was there to interpret. Everyone in that country was young.

The young waitress, who answered to the sweet name of Vaylaravanluanayaluaangrea, was a little intimidated at first. But eventually, lowering her eyes and giving another little bow, she said her friend had told her that she had experienced love as never before with the professor. But what sort of love? asked Hector. (Because there are many sorts of love, which we will explain to you as we go along.) Young Vayla blushed a little and eventually said that her colleague, who was called Not for short, had told her the professor was a tireless lover, which was not new to her, but more importantly he always sensed exactly what she wanted him to do at any given moment. This experience had so amazed the young masseuse that she had decided to follow the professor wherever he went. Hector learnt from her friend Vayla that Not was twenty-three and he remembered the professor was a little over sixty.

Had the professor discovered one of the secrets of love?

He thanked the young woman for all this useful information and went for a dip in the swimming pool. He thought if he tired himself out enough he'd be able to fall asleep without thinking about Clara.

A little later in his room, Hector wrote:

Seedling no. 6: True love is always sensing what the other wants.

At the same time, Hector remembered that this seedling could be quite dangerous. He had seen a lot of people who said to themselves: 'If she really loved me, she would understand without me having to tell her,' and it was quite untrue – sometimes the other person does love you but doesn't understand you very well, and it is best to tell them what you really want.

Seedling no. 7: Love can be wonderful when the other senses what we want, but we must also be able to help them by expressing our desires.

Hector then remembered some women whose desires he had neglected a bit and who had still been very much in love with him. And then he thought of Clara, whom he had been very nice to recently, and who was now wondering whether she was still in love with him. A little angry, he wrote: *You should never pay too much attention to a woman's desires.*

But writing such a thing made him feel sad and he crossed it out. That phrase threatened to upset the harmony in his little seed bed.

But what could he conclude? If you didn't pay enough attention to their desires, they left you and if you paid too much they left you, too. And doubtless the same went for men.

He said to himself that he would like to have a little chat with the professor, and he went back down to the pool.

HECTOR MAKES A GOOD FRIEND

HECTOR wasn't very keen on the idea of going to explore a temple recently cleared of landmines in a region that wasn't safe, but since the professor had visited the temple before he disappeared, he told himself that in the end it was part of his mission to go there looking for clues.

He was thinking about all this in the shade of the trees around the pool while sipping an occasional cocktail from the menu in order not to think about Clara for too long. He wasn't sure now whether to choose the Singapore Sling or the B52. The cocktails and the sight of the pretty waitress who brought them took his mind off things. And he said to himself that if Clara left him he wouldn't really care very much if he got blown up by a landmine. Or else he would go and live in a little house on stilts at the edge of the jungle with the pretty waitress and they would have beautiful children who would sing by the fireside in the evenings. Finally, he settled for the B52.

'I hear you'd like to go to the temple at Benteasaryaramay tomorrow?'

Hector lowered his sunglasses. A rather stocky man running slightly to fat was looking at him, smiling.

He was also wearing a shirt with button-down pockets and long military-looking shorts. In fact, his whole appearance was a bit military, but he said his name was Jean-Marcel and he was a tourist, and what luck because he also wanted to visit the temple recently cleared of landmines.

Hector invited him to sit down and have a drink, and they agreed to hire a car with a driver for their little excursion. Afterwards, they had dinner beside the pool and Jean-Marcel told Hector he was married, and had gone to a neighbouring country on a business trip. He had decided to stop off here on his way back and take another look at the famous temples, all of which he had seen before, except for the one recently cleared of mines, which was apparently very interesting.

As often happens when you are abroad, you talk more easily with your fellow countrymen, and as Hector and Jean-Marcel liked each other, they told each other a bit about their lives. Of course, Hector said he was sightseeing and didn't mention his mission. And all he said about Clara was that she couldn't come with him because of her work, which was true, but not the whole truth. Jean-Marcel was married with two children – a boy and a girl who were already quite grown-up – but Hector sensed he wasn't telling the whole truth either, and he wondered whether Jean-Marcel's wife was really awaiting his return or whether she was fed up with waiting for him, because in fact he spent his whole life travelling on business.

Because you have to get up very early if you want to go sightseeing in hot countries, they soon said good-night to each other.

*

The next day, Hector and Jean-Marcel had difficulty finding a driver as no one would go near the temple. In the end, they found a man who kept laughing all the time, and Hector wondered whether he was quite right in the head. But maybe it was the custom of the country, in which case the driver was normal. But when he saw that all the other drivers were laughing as they watched them drive off he began to get worried.

HECTOR AND THE TEMPLE IN THE JUNGLE

THE country that had been ravaged by crazy leaders was still very beautiful. The road threaded its way through lush countryside full of tall trees and pretty wooden houses on stilts. In the shade of the houses you could see people sleeping in hammocks, women squatting as they did the cooking, children at play, dogs wagging their tails and sometimes cows with a hump on their necks and a tendency to cross the road without looking.

Hector said to himself that this country was very beautiful, but at the same time he knew that its beauty came from its poverty, because the moment it became richer, people would want to have ugly concrete houses with moulded plastic balustrades, like in the neighbouring countries, and minimarkets, factories and hoardings would spring up around all the villages. On the other hand, you couldn't wish it on these people to remain poor.

'That idiot has taken a wrong turning,' said Jean-Marcel.

He was following the map while keeping an eye on the driver, and all credit to him as it isn't easy finding your bearings in a foreign country. He made the driver go back and take the right road because, although he couldn't speak much Khmer, Jean-Marcel was the sort of person who could make himself understood very well.

Then the driver began driving very fast, which wasn't a good idea because of the cows, and Jean-Marcel had to tell him rather loudly to slow down.

'For God's sake, I don't know where they dug this one up!'

'He was the only one who agreed to take us,' said Hector.

The driver began laughing again.

Jean-Marcel and Hector started talking to pass the time. People found it easy to talk to Hector, and so Jean-Marcel explained to him that things weren't so good between him and his wife because she didn't really like him travelling to Asia all the time on business.

'She knows I'm no saint when I'm away from home. But I really don't want to split up with her, I want us to stay together.'

Hector showed him what he had written on the plane:

Seedling no. 5: True love is not being unfaithful (even when you want to be).

'I know,' said Jean-Marcel with a sigh. 'But so long as I'm only getting laid and not having a proper affair, I tell myself I'm not really cheating on my wife. What can I do? It's the way we're made. I know it's nothing to be proud of.'

Hector remembered his own thoughts about the air hostess and the pretty waitress at the hotel, and he agreed that it was nothing to be proud of either.

Just then, Jean-Marcel looked at the driver.

'He's dropping off, the idiot! We need to keep our eye on him, for God's sake!'

The temple stood crumbling in the middle of the forest. In fact it was not so much that the temple was in the middle of the forest as that the forest was in the middle of the temple because a few tall trees had grown through some of the walls and you could even see roots, like giant octopus tentacles, curled around a group of statues.

The driver stopped the car in the shade of a tree and watched Jean-Marcel and Hector walk off and, for some reason which only he knew, this made him laugh.

'I don't know how you say "pain in the neck" in Khmer, but that's what he's giving me,' said Jean-Marcel.

'Maybe it's his way of saying see you later,' said Hector, who was the kind of person who always liked to smooth things out.

They walked along a little path among the trees leading to the temple. Despite the shade, it was beginning to get very hot.

Hector noticed a small stake painted red next to the path.

'That means it's cleared of mines,' said Jean-Marcel. 'Everything's okay.'

Even so, Hector said to himself that the stake wasn't pointing in any direction, and they couldn't know if the ground had been cleared before the stake, after the stake or along the whole path.

'I can see footprints,' said Jean-Marcel, walking ahead, 'so there's no problem.'

Hector told himself that, after all, Jean-Marcel already knew the country and he could be trusted.

They walked into the middle of the ruined temple, taking care anyway to keep to the path.

'Magnificent!' said Jean-Marcel.

And it was true. On the crumbling walls beautiful dancers sculpted in stone smiled mysteriously, no doubt because they knew that with those perfect curves they would never be short of lovers of art. Reading the guide to the region, Hector had understood why Professor Cormorant had wanted to come to this temple: it had been built by a prince who, after getting to know one of the dancers intimately, had dedicated it to love. For a moment, he envisaged Clara's face on the bodies of all the stone dancers, and wondered whether if he built a temple like that just for her she would fall in love with him again. Well, she must still be in love with him a little, mustn't she?

'Over here is very beautiful,' he heard Jean-Marcel's voice say.

Hector carried on along the path and found Jean-Marcel admiring a large doorway that had become a bit lopsided over time.

The palace must have been magnificent when it was newly built, but now, in ruins, it had a still more poignant charm. A bit like a long-lost love, thought Hector.

Jean-Marcel explained, 'This temple was in use for a century then they fought and lost a few wars, and the jungle reclaimed it.'

Hector noticed some more little red stakes amid the ruins.

'Hmm,' said Jean-Marcel, 'it's just for show – they can't have gone to much trouble to clear mines in here; the mines were laid mainly around the temples.'

Hector wondered whether the temple was going to teach him something or whether he had come here for nothing. Perhaps all he had done was discover the splendour of a lost civilisation, like his might be one day, and Martians might visit the ruins of his city and mistake the remains of traffic lights for icons.

He was having difficulty keeping up with Jean-Marcel, who had begun climbing a big flight of steps the sides of which were collapsing, when, suddenly, they heard female voices.

They saw two young Japanese women walking in one of the upper galleries.

'They shouldn't be up there,' said Jean-Marcel.

'Because of the mines?'

'No, because this whole thing is liable to collapse. Even though those Japanese girls don't look too heavy.'

They gestured to them to come down. The young Japanese women jumped when they saw Hector and Jean-Marcel, then made their way back in their direction, taking very small steps in their Nike trainers, which looked bigger than they were, and their little white sunhats.

The two men introduced themselves to Miko, who spoke very good English, and Chizourou, who spoke none at all.

As Hector was a little hot and was beginning to feel quite tired, he stayed in the shade talking to the two young Japanese women, while Jean-Marcel climbed everything it was possible to climb in the temple.

The two women were great friends. As previously mentioned, people found it quite easy to talk to Hector, and Miko explained she had brought Chizourou sightseeing to take her mind off things, because she had recently had her heart broken. Hector looked at young Chizourou, who did have a very sad expression on her pale face. She had almost married a young man whom she loved very much, but he had decided it wasn't a good idea. Why? Because the two of them had done the things people in love do, and afterwards the fiancé thought that if Chizourou was able to do that before she got married she wasn't a responsible girl and he couldn't possibly marry her. And now Chizourou was thinking about him all the time, and this Hector understood.

He tried to find something comforting to say to Chizourou. The first thing he thought of was that a boy who had ideas like that wasn't right for a girl like Chizourou, who was visiting a temple recently cleared of mines in a region that wasn't safe. So she wouldn't have been happy with him anyway. Miko translated for Chizourou, who listened attentively and finally gave a little smile. In the end, her story made Hector think about his opinions on love: why do we go on being in love with someone who makes us suffer? And why do we fall out of love with someone who cares about us? Apparently, even

Japanese women suffered from this problem. Thinking that reminded Hector of Professor Cormorant's message about 'silly cultural prejudices'.

Miko and Chizourou started talking to each other, and then Miko told Hector they had found a strange sculpture – very different from the row of dancers with their mysterious smiles – in a hidden recess of the temple.

Just then, Jean-Marcel came back, and he was also very interested in the strange sculpture. Miko and Chizourou showed them the way. They followed the two Japanese women through a series of passageways, where the sun filtered through huge sculpted windows, and suddenly they came out into the forest. Miko explained that they only needed to walk along the outer wall of the temple and they would come to the sculpture.

'Hmm,' said Jean-Marcel. 'That will take us outside the temple.'

'There are some little red stakes,' said Hector.

'I'm not sure that means much.'

'Well, they've already been that way.'

'Those girls don't weigh much and the ground is soft,' Jean-Marcel said, as though thinking out loud.

They carried on walking. Jean-Marcel took the lead, followed by Hector, Miko and Chizourou. Hector was glad Chizourou hadn't taken the lead, because he thought she might not mind stepping on a mine and wouldn't have been careful enough.

'Is everything all right?' Hector asked Jean-Marcel.

'Yes, yes, everything's okay.'

Even so, Hector noticed Jean-Marcel was looking down at his feet as he walked, and he said to himself that everything wasn't as okay as all that, and maybe it was stupid to be blown up by a mine while sightseeing or even on a mission for a big pharmaceutical company.

But Jean-Marcel began singing, which showed he wasn't too worried. Hector could make out the words:

'If you believe in your destiny
Take your parachute and jump . . .'

And he thought to himself that it wasn't surprising Jean-Marcel had a military appearance.

They reached a small opening in the temple wall and went through it. They came out into a tiny square courtyard, its walls sculpted with the same type of dancer, but one bas-relief was very different from the others.

What amused Hector was that it looked like a very early psychoanalysis session – a woman patient was lying on a couch and the analyst, also a woman, was sitting next to her. Of course, she was sitting on the couch and not in an armchair, and she was also massaging the patient's legs, but as this was the tenth century naturally the technique hadn't yet had time to evolve. The couch resembled a dragon, which might symbolise the patient's neurosis, which she would learn to control thanks to psychoanalysis. Underneath it were numerous fish, turtles and other aquatic animals clearly representing the impulses originating in the depths of the unconscious. On the far left you could see the secretary making appointments.

Hector told himself that if the professor had seen this sculpture he must have found it very interesting.

'Well, there's more,' said Jean-Marcel, 'the tour isn't over yet.'

Hector said he'd prefer to continue contemplating the little courtyard and the early psychoanalysis session. Miko had a word with Chizourou and it was decided that Jean-Marcel and Miko would carry on exploring the temple while Hector and Chizourou sat quietly in the shade.

They heard Jean-Marcel and Miko's footsteps fade into the distance and then there was silence. Chizourou didn't speak any English and Hector spoke no Japanese, and so they just exchanged occasional little smiles to show they appreciated each other's company. Beneath the little white hat, Chizourou's face had an unassuming, innocent beauty suggesting a pleasant nature, and Hector hoped her fiancé would have time to come to his senses, realise his mistake and go back to Chizourou before she in turn stopped loving him. He wondered what Chizourou thought about him, and also whether it was obvious he had taken a shine to her.

Just then, Chizourou puckered her lips and went 'Ooooooh' quite loudly, which made Hector jump. She pointed to a crack in the stone above the early psychoanalysis session. You could see a little piece of bamboo, like the tip of a cane, sticking out. Chizourou had only seen it thanks to a ray of sunlight which suddenly made it stand out against the stone.

Hector wasn't very good at climbing, but scrambling up the sculpted walls wasn't very difficult. He grasped the little piece of bamboo and went back to Chizourou.

She went 'Ooooooh' again when she saw Hector pull a roll of paper out of the bamboo. Hector immediately recognised Professor Cormorant's handwriting.

Dear friend,

This note is a gamble, but then so is conducting a scientific experiment. I knew they would send you in search of me, and that you would learn of my visit to the temple. So I counted on your curiosity to lead you to this sculpture, and if you are reading this note then I was right. I received your message, but you are touchingly naïve if you believe you are the only one who knows that email address. They know everything there is to know about you, and probably a bit more besides.

I am on the brink of making several important discoveries, along with my charming assistant, whom you already know about, and those rotten bastards want to come and spoil everything. To keep them at bay, I must completely cover my tracks, which means severing all communication with you, but I may suddenly need an intermediary like you. Keep sending me emails, but remember I am not the only one reading them, which could be an advantage. In the meantime,

Make haste, my beloved!
And be thou like to a roe or to a young hart upon the mountains of spices.

Kind regards,
Professor Cormorant

HECTOR TAKES RISKS

HECTOR had scarcely finished reading Professor Cormorant's note under Chizourou's inquisitive gaze when they heard Miko's terrified screams coming from outside.

They dashed out of the little courtyard and came to the edge of a grassy path overgrown by trees, which must have been an old moat. There they saw Miko, crying and screaming at the same time, and looking frightened.

Crouched at her feet, Jean-Marcel appeared to be cautiously digging up the soil with his hands.

'Stay where you are,' he shouted to Hector. 'Tell Miko to come over to you.'

Chizourou and Miko had begun talking very fast in Japanese, and this time it was Chizourou who seemed to be comforting Miko.

Hector insisted Miko come over to them but she appeared terror-struck, unable to move. She had seen that Jean-Marcel was dealing with a landmine and she could no longer trust the ground around her.

Eventually, Hector, trying to walk in Miko and Jean-Marcel's footsteps, went over and brought Miko back to Chizourou, whom he had left standing with her feet firmly planted in a big stone doorway.

'That's better,' said Jean-Marcel. 'I don't like being watched while I work.'

Eventually he stood up, holding a small greenish plastic saucer in his hand.

'You can always spot them if you look closely, especially after rain, which brings them up to the surface. But it's very difficult at night.'

Hector wondered when Jean-Marcel would have had the opportunity of walking over a minefield at night – he must have led a very interesting life. But Jean-Marcel continued explaining.

'We're safe now,' he said. 'It takes about thirty kilos of pressure to make this n asty little thing blow up.'

He began unscrewing a sort of stopper on top of the mine and pulled out a little tube and some other small objects and tossed them as far as he could into the forest, and he placed the defused mine on a rock where everyone could see it.

'That'll show them they might need to be a bit more thorough about clearing mines.'

He walked back towards them looking rather pleased with himself. Hector remembered that one of the secrets of happiness was feeling you are doing something useful, and there was no doubt Jean-Marcel had just done something useful.

Chizourou still had her arms round Miko, comforting her, and they were quite touching, the little Japanese girls, as Jean-Marcel called them.

Finally, they decided it was time to go back to their

car; the business with the mine had put a bit of a dampener on their excursion.

Under the tree, their driver had fallen asleep behind the wheel with all the doors open because it was very hot.

The young Japanese girls went 'Ooooooh' again. Miko explained they had also hired a car with a driver, but he wasn't there any more – he must have left without them.

'I don't like the look of this,' said Jean-Marcel.

'Neither do I,' said Hector.

Having avoided the mines, they were now possibly going to be exposed to the other danger in that beautiful region: bad people. The crazy leaders who had nearly destroyed that country were no longer in power, but some of their troops had taken refuge in the forest where they still lived, growing rich from trafficking various things: drugs that were grown nearby, precious stones that almost flowed out of the earth, or young girls whom they treated as merchandise. From time to time, they kidnapped people passing through and demanded ransom money, and sometimes they killed them, although that didn't happen very often as the new army in their country came down hard on them, which was bad for business. So the risk of death was very slight (as slight as stumbling on a mine in a temple cleared of mines). But Miko and Chizourou's driver had left without them and this sudden flight might mean he knew something, unlike Hector and Jean-Marcel's driver who woke up laughing because, as Jean-Marcel said, he was an idiot.

HECTOR IS THOUGHTFUL

In the car, just to occupy his mind, Hector began to think about love again. He was in the back with Miko and Chizourou, while Jean-Marcel sat next to the driver and watched the road very attentively.

Hector was thinking about his feelings towards the air hostess who had brought him champagne, and also about the fact that Jean-Marcel couldn't manage to be a saint when he was travelling in that region. It was nothing to be proud of, but it was still part of love – feeling desire for someone you scarcely know and don't necessarily want to get to know, except to do what people do when they are in love, although love didn't come into it in this case.

The countryside was as beautiful on the way back as it had been on the way there, but the thought that the region was unsafe made everything appear threatening. Even the cows seemed to be watching them slyly as they went past.

Sexual desire was clearly part of love, but it wasn't everything. What were the sure signs that you loved someone?

Jean-Marcel took a small pair of binoculars out of his bag.

Hector thought about Clara. He missed her. That was love, missing the other person when they were far away. But Hector also remembered that when he was a child and his parents left him at summer camp he missed them a lot to begin with. (He felt better after a couple of days because he made friends.) So missing people was also an element in non-sexual love.

The car braked sharply, interrupting his thoughts – a cow had just crossed the road without looking, and Jean-Marcel shouted a stream of abuse at it, which luckily neither Miko nor Chizourou could understand.

Sometimes, you could also miss someone you loved almost exclusively sexually. Hector remembered having both male and female patients who would say things like: 'We have nothing to say to one another of any interest, but as soon as we're in bed . . .'

It was a bit like a drug you'd like to stop taking, but which you can't live without and it creates a real need.

He opened his little notebook and wrote:

Seedling no. 8: Sexual desire is essential to love.

He knew there were also couples who loved each other deeply and who hardly ever made love, even though it wasn't at all fashionable to say so nowadays. He added: *but not always.*

Seedling no. 9: Needing the other is a sign of love.

Just then, he saw Jean-Marcel speaking into his portable phone, which looked bigger than an ordinary mobile, then he quickly put it back in his bag. Hector had time to glimpse a black metallic object in the bag as he did so.

'Is everything all right?' he asked.

'There's no signal here,' said Jean-Marcel.

And yet Hector had the impression Jean-Marcel had said a few words into the phone.

A few seconds later, he saw a helicopter fly overhead before disappearing.

He remembered the hotel offered it as a way of visiting the temple, but friends had always told him there were countries where you should never go in a helicopter, and this was one of them.

He thought again of Clara and the jokes they had made about the crabs on the beach back on the island. At that moment, neither of them had felt desire, nor had they been missing each other because they were together. And yet it had been an intensely happy moment and they had laughed at the same things. How could you describe that kind of love?

Miko asked him what he was writing in his notebook, and Hector explained he was writing down some thoughts about love. Miko explained this to Chizourou and they both looked intrigued. Hector had noticed that girls everywhere liked to talk about love, whereas boys didn't always. Hector asked her what the clearest sign of being in love was in Japan.

Chizourou and Miko talked for a moment and then said that the clearest sign of love is when you miss the other person and think about him or her all the time.

Yet another argument against silly cultural prejudices, Professor Cormorant would have said.

HECTOR SUFFERS

Dear Hector,

It makes me sad after our last conversation to think of you alone and so far away. I'm really sorry, I should have waited until you got back to talk about us, but you kept questioning me, and I ended up telling you everything that was bothering me. And now you've gone, I'm wondering whether it was a good thing to have told you I was no longer sure about my feelings towards you. I do still love you, otherwise I wouldn't be missing you now, but, at the same time, and I'm sorry if this hurts, I have the feeling we can't be a couple any more. I see you as part of my family, but not as my future husband or the father of my children. And yet the thought of never seeing you again is incredibly painful, and part of me wants to hold on to you – as a friend, some would say, but that word is inadequate; I feel closer to you than I do to anyone else in the whole world, and that's without even mentioning all your amazing qualities.

You'll think I'm blowing hot and cold, that I don't know what I want, and no doubt there's some truth in that. We've known each other for a long time and we've already had our ups and downs. There was a time when I wanted us to get married, but I remember you being the one who wasn't very keen on starting a family. By saying this to you I feel you will fret and blame yourself for having let the moment pass. Don't torture yourself – that's life – we don't choose our feelings and we can't blame ourselves or others for them.

You are still the most important person in my life, even though I can't see us being together any more. It's dreadful – each time I say this I feel as if I am punishing you, and yet we've always been honest with one another.

Take care, keep safe, and tell yourself that whatever happens you are still my Hector.

Love and kisses.

Hector finished his vodka amaretto and waited for the pretty waitress in the sarong to bring him the next one. It was growing dark beside the pool and he wondered how he was going to fill his time while avoiding thinking about Clara. He was trying to do exactly that when he recognised a few melancholy notes in the background music coming from the bar; it was a song he had listened to with Clara, and which just then he was terrified of hearing:

I no longer love you, my darling, I no longer love you till the end of time.
I no longer love you, my darling, I no longer love you till the end of time.

And those sweet strains began to break Hector's heart. Just then, Jean-Marcel turned up, not looking very happy either. He sat down without paying any attention to the song and explained that he had just spoken to his wife on the phone.

'Do you think two people who have loved each other can stop loving each other?' he asked Hector.

Hector said he feared it was possible, yes. And he thought about Professor Cormorant's drugs. Was there one that allowed people to go on loving each other for as long as they wanted?

'I have a feeling it's over between me and my wife,' said Jean-Marcel, 'and yet we used to be so happy together.'

They ordered a bottle of white wine because cocktails are a bit sickly after a while.

Jean-Marcel and Hector began comparing notes on women, which is always a good way for men to become friends quickly.

'They never know what they want.'

'And they're never happy.'

'As soon as we're nice to them, they make us pay.'

'The worst thing is their friends' advice.'

'They always want to control us, and once they've succeeded they lose interest.'

Finally, after the second bottle, they decided to go out on the town and ordered a tuk-tuk, which is a local type of rickshaw, except that instead of a bicycle it is a scooter pulling two fat white people while a less fat less white person drives.

It was quite pleasant driving through the night air after the heat of the day. The streets were fairly quiet, with just a few cars and some dogs, although you could see several bars lit up and some massage parlours with flashing neon signs. Apparently, the people in that town needed round-the-clock massages, perhaps because of the tiring visits to the temples. But Hector remembered what the hotel manager had said and he realised they weren't only giving ordinary massages.

Finally the tuk-tuk dropped them at a bar where a few young Western men were drinking and chatting with some young women who were unmistakably Asian.

Two of the women immediately came over to talk to them. They wanted Hector and Jean-Marcel to buy them a drink, and in return they seemed willing to keep repeating how handsome they were and trying to find out the name of their hotel. They smiled, showing all their pretty teeth, but in their eyes Hector glimpsed less happy things. Younger brothers and sisters who needed food. A drug dealer who was owed money. Medicines that had to be paid for.

Hector and Jean-Marcel looked at one another.

'I'm not in the mood,' said Jean-Marcel.

'Neither am I,' said Hector.

They climbed back into the tuk-tuk and Jean-Marcel was clearly quite drunk because he couldn't get in on his first attempt.

'Kerls, kerls!' said the driver.

Hector didn't understand Khmer; he just said 'hotel' and dozed off a little while making sure Jean-Marcel didn't fall over the side.

Finally, the tuk-tuk dropped them at another place, a rather dimly lit sort of shed, where a few local men were waiting around in armchairs. Hector and Jean-Marcel were glad of the armchairs, which were a lot more comfortable than the hard seats in the tuk-tuk. The first thing Hector noticed was that they were the only white men there, and then that some young girls were sitting opposite them on plastic chairs under a bright light. They looked like schoolgirls; they wore jeans and brand-name T-shirts, like in Hector's country, and high-heeled sandals that showed their pretty toes, and some were using their mobiles while others talked or stared into space with bored expressions. Hector wondered why all the young girls were sitting on one side and the men on the other, and why the lights were so bright that some of them were blinking in the glare, and then suddenly he understood.

He saw that some of the girls stared at him and flashed him little smiles, while others, on the contrary, looked scared and hid their faces as soon as he looked at them. They seemed so young; already women, but still young enough to be at school or watch the pop charts on television. In Hector's country, they would have been studying or working as shop assistants or trainees. Some of them reminded him of his friends' daughters, or some of his young patients. They talked among themselves just like girls their age anywhere.

Hector saw Jean-Marcel was watching them, too. He remembered Jean-Marcel telling him his daughter was sixteen.

Hector and Jean-Marcel looked at each other again, stood up and walked back to the tuk-tuk.

'Kerls? Kerls? . . . Poys?' screeched the driver.

'Hotel! Hotel! Hotel!' Jean-Marcel said, a little too loudly, Hector thought.

The driver also had a family to feed and commissions to earn from the clients he brought.

Later, in his room, looking through his notebook, Hector reread:

Seedling no. 8: Sexual desire is an essential part of love,

which he had decided wasn't true for everybody, nor at all times.

He thought of the girls sitting under the lights and he wrote:

Seedling no. 10: Men's sexual desire can create many hells.

Hector thought of the local men sitting next to him, who took their time before choosing, or only fantasised because they didn't have enough money to pay for half an hour of a young girl's beauty, and of all the frustrated men in his own country who might have dreamt of being in a place like that, and of himself (because who knows what might have happened if he had gone there on a different night having drunk a bit less or a bit more or without Clara on his mind?), and it made him think again of old François's words. What if somebody found a way of suppressing sexual desire? Wouldn't life be nicer and more decent?

HECTOR MAKES A CHOICE

JUST as Hector was dropping off to sleep, there was a knock at his door. He turned on his bedside light and walked barefoot across the smooth, varnished acacia-wood floor, and opened the door. The young waitress with the complicated name was standing there, as pretty as ever in her sarong, and once again she gave him a graceful oriental bow. She looked nervous. Hector gestured to her to come in.

He was very surprised. He hadn't rung for anything, and, besides, it was only in novels that enchanting young women came to knock on your bedroom door at night. As she walked past him, the pretty waitress handed him an envelope. Hector invited her to sit down in one of the armchairs, which she did, crossing her legs underneath her. In the light of the bedside lamp, her face had a beautiful amber glow and her supple figure and her smile gave the impression that one of the stone dancers had stepped off the temple wall under cover of darkness and come all the way to his room. She looked at him without saying anything and he felt a bit uneasy.

He opened the envelope. As he had suspected, it was a letter from Professor Cormorant.

Dear friend,

I left another message for you in the temple, which I trust you found, warning you that everything you do is being watched, including any emails you send from anywhere. That is why I have chosen a charming messenger, the gentle Vayla, to deliver this letter to you, in the certainty that, like Caesar's wife, she would never be suspected.

My dear friend, you are now going to be part of my experiment, assuming you have the courage. If you take part, you will be contributing not only to a major scientific advance, but to the beginning of a revolution in the history of humanity, which will transform our customs, culture, art and most probably our economy too. Imagine how different the world would be if we could harness the power of love!

But let's not get carried away; this is only a preliminary stage and I myself am still fumbling about, if you'll pardon the expression.

I have entrusted the charming Vayla with two small phials containing a solution of two different drugs. I invite you both to go somewhere quiet and take them together. You have nothing to fear. I carried out the experiment on myself and as you can see from the tone of this letter I am still in full possession of my faculties. Only, in order to convince my dear Not, who was not entirely persuaded by the methods of Western science, we took my potion at sunrise in the ruins of the temple of love you visited. We spent several very peaceful, and at the same time very intense, hours there, which she enjoyed, and although my poor knowledge of Khmer and her ignorance of English limited our verbal communication, it fortunately left room for other types of communication and an emotional intimacy to which a common language can so often be an impediment.

In order that you do not suffer the side effects which I noticed – and which that prude of a hotel manager probably described to you – I have changed the proportions in the solution: less sexual desire, more emotion and empathy. Also, should you wish to avoid developing an inconvenient attachment to the lovely Vayla, I have developed a third drug designed to wipe out all emotional traces of the experiment. I was able to produce it in tablet form. If you decide to take it, I naturally recommend you give half to your partner, so that she won't be left pining for evermore after your departure. As for me, I haven't taken the antidote, because I say to myself that, at my age, my lovely, gentle companion is undoubtedly the best thing I could hope for in life. And what of conversation? you will ask. I am no longer interested in conversing, except with a handful of my colleagues and with you. And so . . .

Thou hast ravished my heart, my sister, my spouse,
Thou hast ravished my heart with one of thine eyes,
With one chain of thy neck.

Well, dear friend, I imagine you reading this letter, while at your feet the lovely Vayla awaits your decision, ready to obey and to please you. Frankly, the stories her friend must have told her about her experiences with me will already have enticed her, not to mention your own personal charm, which I do not underestimate.

You will easily find the clue to my next destination and our next possible meeting place – you just have to be able to read!

Best wishes,
Chester G. Cormorant

Hector folded the letter and found Vayla gazing up at him, and he saw in her eyes a look of expectation and trust that he had rarely seen in a human being. Still sitting cross-legged, she was holding in her palm two small cylindrical phials, each about the size of a pen top.

Hector was in torment. He felt a bit like Snowy when he has to choose between carrying a vital message in his mouth or dropping it in order to seize the delicious bone he has just dug up, and his conscience struggles with a miniature Snowy-devil on one side and a miniature Snowy-angel on the other, each doing their best to win him over. In Hector's case, the message he had to hold on to was his love for Clara, and the wonderfully tempting bone was Vayla, willing to give herself up to him and to the raptures her friend had described.

But suddenly the letter he was holding reminded him of the one Clara had written to him.

I have the feeling we can't be a couple any more.

He took the twin phials from Vayla's hand. She smiled at him and hugged him tenderly round the legs.

HECTOR MAKES LOVE

LATER, when he was almost asleep, Hector was thinking that Professor Cormorant had made a fitting choice in quoting verses from the Song of Songs in his messages. That poem expressed so perfectly what he felt with Vayla and what the professor must have experienced with his new friend.

In the course of a few hours, Hector had experienced with Vayla a range of emotions he hadn't often felt for the same person: intense sexual excitement, it has to be said, accompanied by a rush of tenderness and affection towards her. And when she wanted him to be more forceful than gentle or at other moments more gentle than forceful, Hector sensed it, all the while feeling this surge of tenderness towards her that was as powerful as his desire. When Vayla stared deep into his eyes, he saw she was experiencing the same intense emotions. As they soared together, borne aloft by the mounting current of their love, Hector could not help asking himself questions. What would it be like when they came down? (Don't forget that Hector is a psychiatrist, and he has a tendency to analyse his and other people's feelings, even in the thick of things.)

What memories, what emotional impressions would he and Vayla have of these moments?

Luckily, the professor had come up with an antidote that would allow them to dissolve the bond that now bound them together, like melting a chain link that has been forged in a furnace.

Hector looked at Vayla, lying naked, her eyes closed, a smile on her gently pouting lips. With her arms half raised either side of her head, her legs turned outward and resting flat on the bed, she was like a living replica of one of the stone dancers – *apsara*, as he had been told they were called – decorating the temple walls. No doubt one of her ancestors had posed as a model and, since in that country nobody travelled much, that harmony had been passed on through the generations only to end up next to him on that bed. Psychiatry is interesting, but travelling isn't bad either, thought Hector.

Vayla opened her eyes, smiled and stretched her arms out towards him. Hector knew immediately what he had to do, but he would probably have known that even without the professor's drug.

Later, dawn came. The jungle around the hotel was alive with the squawks of countless birds, and even the odd plaintive *ou-ou-ou* which seemed to suggest the presence of monkeys.

Hector and Vayla had a few more spells of waking and sleeping, and soon it was midday, the sun was high in the sky and the jungle had gone quiet.

The phone rang. It was Jean-Marcel.

'Is everything okay?' he asked.

Hector looked at Vayla's profile as she slept.

'Couldn't be better,' he said.

Even so, he was afraid; he felt a deep desire to protect Vayla for the rest of her life, to be near her always, to make love to her until his dying breath. He felt swept away by a flood he was powerless to resist.

'Shall we have lunch?' Jean-Marcel said.

'Sure.'

He must wake up completely and take the antidote quickly and make Vayla take it with him. He felt her arms on his shoulders.

He turned round and immersed himself in her eyes and her smile, at once delighted and terrified by the emotion he felt, which he sensed she was experiencing at the exact same moment, a look of wonder in her eyes, her heart pounding against his chest.

They mustn't delay in taking the antidote. He couldn't tie her to him nor could he be tied to her.

But when Hector asked her, using gestures, about the professor's promised antidote, Vayla looked puzzled. She appeared not to understand.

Hector picked up the hotel biro and notepad and drew two small phials, and next to them an oval-shaped pill. Vayla gazed at his drawing intently, like a young fawn seeing a rabbit for the first time. Hector drew a round pill. Vayla blushed slightly. She looked at Hector and then showed him her slender fingers.

He understood: she thought he had drawn a wedding ring.

Hector drew pills of every possible shape – triangular, rectangular, pear-shaped, heart-shaped, in the shape of a four-leafed clover – and even made one out of a piece of scrunched-up paper, but he only succeeded in making Vayla laugh – perhaps she thought he was doing it to amuse her. And Hector couldn't help laughing when he saw her laugh, and at the same time he was thinking that the real joker was the professor.

He hadn't given Vayla the antidote. Or perhaps there was no antidote.

Now he really had to find Professor Cormorant.

HECTOR HAS A REST

'You look great!' said Jean-Marcel.

'I think this climate agrees with me.'

Jean-Marcel started laughing. 'You must be the first!'

They had lunch in the shade of the bar, and waitresses who looked peculiarly like Vayla brought them salads or little sandwiches. In the swimming pool light-skinned children played with their darker-skinned nannies. Jean-Marcel kept his sunglasses on in the shade and looked rather pale despite his generally healthy appearance.

Hector was thinking about Vayla. She had crept out of his room earlier. Hector hadn't understood where she was going, but clearly she couldn't be seen with a guest. He had a burning desire to see her again while at the same time thinking how crazy it all was. And what if there were no antidote? Must he spend the rest of his life beside these temples? Or take Vayla to his country?

'Will you be visiting any other temples?' asked Jean-Marcel.

'No, I won't actually,' said Hector. 'I've seen everything I wanted to see. How about you?'

'I'm not sure. I'm thinking about it.'

'In any case, I enjoyed our outing yesterday. And well done for that lesson in mine clearance!'

'Oh,' Jean-Marcel said, shrugging his shoulders, 'that was nothing. The mine wasn't even booby-trapped.'

'Booby-trapped?'

Jean-Marcel explained that sometimes they didn't only lay a mine so that it exploded when you stepped on it, they also connected it by a wire to a second mine underneath so that when the bomb disposal expert lifted up the first mine, the second one exploded in his face, which was only a figure of speech since the moment it exploded he no longer had a face.

It always depressed Hector a little hearing about all the things men were able to invent in order to harm others. He imagined the nice engineer going home every evening and tucking his children into bed while he read them a bedtime story, then discussing with his nice wife whether they should move so each child could have their own bedroom, and then, before going to bed, preparing a bit for the next day's meeting where he had to make an impressive PowerPoint presentation of his new mine, containing just the right amount of explosive to blow someone's foot off, because carrying a wounded soldier slowed down and demoralised a patrol far more than a dead soldier, not to mention his screams making them easier to locate. All that ingenuity and energy devoted to doing harm when, with Professor Cormorant's drugs, people could, on the contrary, devote their energy to doing themselves and others good.

Of course, a nation that had such drugs at its disposal would no longer really want to wage war; everyone would prefer to stay at home and go on loving one another. Those drugs wouldn't be very good for national defence.

'And where did you learn all this?' Hector asked Jean-Marcel.

'When I was doing my military service,' said Jean-Marcel. 'I was in the Engineers. Laying mines, clearing mines. Assorted tricks, really.'

And, suddenly, who should they see arriving at another table but Miko and Chizourou! Mind you, it wasn't surprising since they were staying at the same hotel.

They came over to say hello and Hector and Jean-Marcel, who were proper gentlemen, invited them to sit at their table.

They still looked very pretty, even without their white sunhats. In fact they looked like two adorable squirrels with their almond-shaped eyes and auburn hair. They ordered kebabs with a Japanese name: *teriyaki*.

They exchanged a few guttural sounds in Japanese and then Miko asked Hector what was written on the piece of paper they had found at the temple. Damn, Chizourou must have told her about their discovery.

'It was a lover's note,' said Hector. '"Chester and Rosalyn were here and their love will last forever."'

He wished he hadn't said the name Chester, which was Professor Cormorant's first name, but he'd been forced to improvise and it had just slipped out.

'What note is that?' asked Jean-Marcel.

Hector explained, and added that it must be a new trend that might catch on at the temple of love: leaving notes, rather like at a Buddhist shrine.

'Didn't you keep it?' asked Jean-Marcel.

'No, I must have lost it in all the excitement over the mine, and then I forgot about it.'

It was true – leading Miko away from the mine had distracted him and he couldn't remember what he'd done with the piece of paper, which, after all, wasn't that important.

'Will their wish come true if their note is no longer in the wall?'

'I expect it's the intention that counts,' said Hector.

Miko and Chizourou started talking again, and then Miko explained that Chizourou had replaced the note in the bamboo and the bamboo in the wall. In Japan, people don't leave things lying on the ground and they respect temple offerings.

'I think I'll stay on for a day or two,' Jean-Marcel said, 'and visit a few temples.'

Chizourou looked more cheerful than she had the day before, and as it turned out, although she didn't speak English, she did speak a little bit of Hector and Jean-Marcel's language.

'Une toute petit peu,' she said.

'And where will you two go next?' Hector asked.

They didn't know yet. Maybe to China. And what did they do for a living in Japan?

Miko explained that they both worked for a big non-governmental organisation whose aim was to protect everything that might be destroyed in the world, including endangered animals, but also ancient temples, and rivers that were as yet unpolluted. Her job was to raise money for restoring the temples; as for Chizourou, she did beautiful drawings of the ruins to convince people their donations were needed. This didn't surprise Hector, who had immediately sensed that Chizourou had a deeply artistic nature.

Without really paying attention, Jean-Marcel and Hector began using their charms a little on these two pretty Japanese girls, who seemed to be having a great time.

Just then, a waitress who looked like Vayla came over to them, a surly expression on her face. In fact it was Vayla, dressed in her hotel waitress's uniform, that's to say in a shimmering orange sarong.

Hector had learnt during his studies that facial expressions are universal (another blow to silly cultural prejudices, the professor would have said) and he could see immediately that Vayla was rather upset.

Jean-Marcel looked impressed. 'Wow, you're a quick worker!'

'Beginner's luck,' said Hector.

Vayla marched off and, without her saying a word, Hector understood she would be meeting him in his room very shortly. But that didn't solve his problem, far from it. In any case, if Professor Cormorant's drug stimulated love it did nothing to suppress jealousy. But was that such a surprise? Weren't love and jealousy inextricably linked? Before saying goodbye to Miko and Chizourou, who were also slightly surprised by the appearance of the furious Vayla, like some angry goddess who could strike you dead with a glance, Hector had time to write down in his little notebook.

Seedling no. 11: Love and jealousy go hand in hand.

HECTOR IS ABLE TO READ

On waking, Hector made out a tiny little tattoo behind Vayla's ear, next to her hairline, so minute he could only read it because he was pressed up close to her. Oddly, they weren't squiggly Khmer letters so much as characters like those on his beautiful Chinese panel. When he looked more closely, he could see it wasn't a tattoo, but a drawing in very dark ink. He woke Vayla up and, using gestures, asked her what the tattoo signified. Yet again, she seemed not to understand, which was becoming a little irritating even if Hector did love her very much, and so he took her by the arm and led her into the bathroom. Vayla seemed even more surprised than he to discover this tiny drawing behind her ear. Hector remembered the professor's message. *You just have to be able to read . . .*

He very carefully copied the characters out on a piece of writing paper, while Vayla, who was keen to get rid of the mysterious tattoo, waited, stamping her feet impatiently.

In the hotel bar, a few Chinese men wearing Lacoste shirts, gold glasses and Pierre Cardin belts were drinking beer and talking in quite loud voices. Hector showed them the copied-out text. The Chinese men passed it to each other, laughing.

One of them explained. The first two characters meant *Shanghai*, the following ones referred to a bird. The Chinese men didn't know its name in English, but it was a diver with a long beak that fed off saltwater and freshwater fish . . .

Now Hector knew where to find Professor Cormorant. Although not exactly, since he had gone into hiding in a city with sixteen million inhabitants.

HECTOR TAKES TO THE AIR AGAIN

Vayla was sleeping with her head on his shoulder while he watched the lights of Shanghai stretching into the distance, like a vast Milky Way in the process of being created, as their plane calmly flew overhead.

Hector had not forgotten Clara, but what he was experiencing with Vayla made him think a lot about love. After all, this was an experiment, Professor Cormorant had said, and he needed to note down some observations.

He had intended leaving Vayla behind and continuing his journey alone. He would have shown her how to set up an email account and they would have been able to send each other messages and photos. But when he had begun explaining this, with the aid of a few little drawings, he had seen such despair on Vayla's face, so unlike her sweet *apsara's* smile, that he hadn't had the heart to continue.

And now he could feel her breath on his neck; she was leaning against him, sleeping, with the innocence of a child that knows she will never be abandoned.

Hector opened his notebook and wrote:

I didn't have the courage to leave Vayla. Why? Because all suffering related to abandonment upsets me?

Hector had learnt this when he was a young psychiatrist and had himself gone to lie on the couch of an older psychiatrist to talk to him about his mother and other things. He had a problem with abandonment; he found it difficult to bear (look at the business with Clara) and even more difficult to inflict on others. All of which can make your love life very complicated.

Was I the one who was afraid of not being able to bear her absence?

That same problem of abandonment. Would he have to lie down and talk about it again, possibly on old François's couch this time?

Have I become sexually dependent on her?

That question of sexual obsession again – we won't dwell on it; it's easy enough to understand.

Have the professor's drugs created an attachment between us?

Have our experiences together created an attachment?

Because, take note, Hector and Vayla had not only experienced sexual emotion (although that had taken up a lot of their time).

They had already made each other sad when Hector had wanted to leave Vayla behind and he saw her eyes fill with tears. And they had made each other angry, too. She had been angry when she had stood, like a wrathful goddess, next to the two Japanese girls. And Hector had been angry later on.

This is how it happened: before they left, Hector, his suitcase packed, was waiting in his room for Vayla, who didn't come. Hector began to wonder whether she had decided to stay behind with her family after all.

And then she had shown up, completely transformed. Vayla was dressed up like an adolescent out of a pop video; her hair was all frizzy, she was wearing frayed bell-bottom jeans, a sequined T-shirt, wedge sandals, and she stood there in front of him proud as a peacock. To top it all she was clutching a handbag, a copy of an expensive brand from Hector's country.

Hector felt a rush of anger, the same as he would if he saw a supermarket inside a temple or a publicity hoarding hanging from a statue. He wasn't sure whether to be angry with himself and his society for destroying what was beautiful about everybody else's, or with Vayla for having sabotaged her own beauty, but in any case it was not her fault. She soon found herself naked under the shower, in tears in spite of Hector's best attempts to console her – not easy when you don't speak the same language. Later, he helped her choose some silk outfits at the hotel boutique.

To begin with, Vayla seemed shocked by the numbers on the price tags. No, no, she shook her head at Hector, horrified, no doubt, because for her that sum of money was enough to support her family for several months, but she quite quickly became used to the idea, and all at Gunther's expense.

Through the shop window, Hector noticed the hotel manager standing in the lobby looking at them with a funny expression on his face. A masseuse and a waitress both in the same week – he must have been anticipating a serious staff shortage.

But the people in reception dealt with Vayla's visa very efficiently, so we'll tell you the name of the hotel as a thank you: Victoria.

And now on the plane Hector saw her open her eyes in the half-light and lean cautiously over to the window, as though she were a bit nervous of all that emptiness below them, and this was when he told himself he loved her, and it was a catastrophe.

PROFESSOR CORMORANT'S LETTER

Dear friend,

Strictly speaking I shouldn't tell you anything about this experiment as you are the subject of it, although if I may say so you are no ordinary subject, you are practically one of us, and it's not every day you find a qualified psychiatrist to use as a guinea pig. (Perhaps that's one of the things genetic engineering has in store for us: hamsters with modified brains that will make good and inexpensive psychotherapists.)

As you know, a fair amount of research is being done on the biology of love. I would venture to say that I am at the forefront of this research. Let me explain where the other slowcoaches have got to.

They are particularly interested in two natural neurotransmitters: oxytocin and dopamine. It would appear our brains secrete oxytocin at critical moments of our attachment to another being: when mothers breastfeed their babies, when we have sex with someone we love, or simply hold that person in our arms, or when healthy subjects are shown babies or cute baby animals. It is the hormone of love and attachment.

There is a small prairie vole which has a high number of oxytocin receptors in its brain. As a result, the male becomes attached to the female and mates with her for life.

In contrast, his mountain cousin, who has fewer receptors, is a first-class womaniser. However, if we suppress the oxytocin receptors in the former and inject the latter with oxytocin, their behaviours are reversed! (Note that no one took an interest in the female voles' reaction to their modified mates, which might at least have interesting ramifications in terms of marriage guidance.)

So much for gentle oxytocin, let us now turn to that prize bitch dopamine. Every time we experience a pleasurable feeling, dopamine is released in bursts; it is our brain's highest reward, and its secretion is stimulated primarily by novelty; it is the hormone of ever more and ever newer experiences. When we first fall in love, the discovery of a new partner releases a flood of dopamine. The problem is our dopamine receptors then become gradually desensitised, which is why, according to some killjoy authors, passion wanes after eighteen to thirty-six months of living together. At that moment, if nice oxytocin hasn't taken over and created a strong attachment, dopamine drives us to look elsewhere, like poodles on heat.

In point of fact, if we raise the level of this debate, and what pleasure it gives me to do so with you, my dear friend, I would call oxytocin a saint and dopamine a slut! (Note that I do not use the word whore, because some whores are saints, like the famous Mary Magdalene, the only female apostle, who became devoted to one man and one cause.) Oxytocin is a Judaeo-Christian hormone or, if you prefer, a Buddhist hormone: promoting love of your fellow man, faithfulness, the desire to protect others and make them happy, while dopamine is unmistakably the hormone of the devil and temptation, which compels us to break tender emotional bonds in order to get laid, to overindulge in a variety of drugs, and also to go in search of the new, to discover unknown continents, to create marvels, to build a tower of Babel instead of living in harmony, loving one another and breaking home-baked bread together. A philosopher, of course, could churn out hundreds of complicated pages for us on the subject of this duality, but in all modesty I think I have covered the basic elements.

Other ingredients also play a role in desire, but I shall stop here because this message will be read by you-know-who and I don't intend to do their work for them.

All my current research consists of perfecting the modified forms of these active ingredients in order to make their effects last but without the receptors becoming desensitised. I was working with an excellent chemist; unfortunately he increased the dosage in the hope of being able to continue satisfying the appetites of a young research assistant twenty years his junior. Vanity, all is vanity.

Well, dear friend, explaining to you what I know by heart is already beginning to bore me, and perhaps you, too, because, you see, I adore novelty and my dopamine always gets the better of me.

Oxytocinely yours,
Chester G. Cormorant

Hector felt compelled to write, with a slightly heavy heart:

Seedling no. 12: Passion fades after two or three years of living together.

This also reminded him of all those passionate love affairs that lasted for years, or even decades, between two people who weren't able to see each other very often. When one of them was married, for instance. When you can only manage to meet for love and conversation, it takes years to reach the equivalent of three years of living together. At the same time, it feels a bit false compared to the spouse you wake up next to every morning, and who has lost some of his or her allure. Hector had a sudden insight into all the love affairs he had heard about or experienced in his life, and he wrote:

Seedling no. 13: Passion in love can be terribly unfair.

HECTOR AND THE JADE BEAM

Dear Hector,

You didn't reply to my last message. I'm getting worried. I hope you aren't feeling too sad. Gunther seems worried, which makes me think he hasn't heard from you either.

Here life goes on as before. Where are you?

Write back soon.

Lots of love.

Apparently, Clara had a problem with abandonment, too.

Hector was thinking this while looking at a very beautiful, remarkably pale Chinese woman calmly impaling herself on the enormous veined member of a fat Chinaman with a slightly distant look on his face. Actually it was a statue, because they were in a museum, the museum of love to be precise, where thousands of works on the subject had been amassed, further proof that people who have sex on the brain are nothing new.

Faced with the vastness of Shanghai, Hector had decided to start by visiting this museum, telling himself that the professor might also have come here and left him a clue.

They went from room to room, Vayla's arm gently entwined in his, discovering paintings or statues entitled *The Butterfly in Search of Nectar* or *Break Open the Rock so the Spring May Burst Forth* or *The Restless Bird Discovers the Way through the Forest*, because Chinese civilisation is a great civilisation that sees poetry in everything. Hector remembered that a great Chinese leader had even launched a massive campaign known as the Hundred Flowers Movement when it would have been more accurate to call it the Slaughter Anyone Who Stands Out Movement.

He was unable to share these thoughts with Vayla, just as she was unable to understand any of the captions in Chinese and English, but the meaning of the works was fairly explicit, so much so that Hector wondered whether Vayla might not get ideas about the normal size of a, well, of what artists there called 'the jade beam'.

Vayla had laughed with her hand over her mouth when she saw the first pieces, and had then examined the following ones with interest, but gradually it became obvious she was getting bored, and was covering her mouth now in order to yawn. Hector remembered this was a slight difference between men and women. Men were always a little aroused by the image of people making love, as he was at that moment in fact, whereas in general it wasn't enough to put women in the mood – with a few exceptions, but we won't be giving out any phone numbers.

They came to some showcases containing various artefacts carved from ivory. At first glance you might have thought they were pieces of jewellery, but they weren't;

they were accessories and implements designed to console women in the absence of men or to provide men with the extra means to satisfy their women, which proved that even the ancient Chinese had definite feminist sensibilities. Vayla stood transfixed in front of these objects then turned to Hector, cupping her hands behind her ears and moving her head from side to side in imitation of an elephant. She had understood what the objects were carved out of because there were still quite a few elephants in her country, and sometimes even on the roads, instead of a row of heavy trucks, you had to overtake a row of elephants, which is less dangerous because a good elephant never pulls out unexpectedly.

Around them, other visitors chuckled as they viewed the works, and this made Hector wonder: why did the same act, which caused so many to despair because they couldn't do it with the person they wanted to, or as many times as they wanted to, make more or less everyone laugh? Everyone who passed through the museum, including Chinese, Europeans, Americans and others of uncertain origin, laughed or giggled a little when they discovered *The Hungry Horse Gallops towards its Manger* or *The Weary Dragons Repose in Mid-combat*.

Probably, thought Hector, because love is a private emotion. But when you see other people in a frenzy over love, becoming as oblivious to reason as animals or little children, it makes you laugh. Just like it does when you see animals or little children who don't know how to hide their desires under a façade of good manners. Good manners are after all meant to serve as a façade, and love and good manners don't always go together, if you follow.

Hector stood staring at a painting entitled *The Long-necked Cormorant Shoots out a Jet of Foam*, and in this case we don't need to do a drawing for you.

The strange thing about this minuscule painting was that it didn't appear to be in the same style as the others, even though the frame looked older, if anything. To Vayla's astonishment, Hector turned the painting over and found a label with a number printed on it in very fine handwriting – 316 715 9243 – followed by the same ideograms he had read behind Vayla's ear.

Professor Cormorant seemed to be having a lot of fun.

HECTOR AND VAYLA VISIT THE ZOO

When Hector and Vayla arrived at Shanghai Zoo (the meeting place suggested by Professor Cormorant, whom Hector had called at the number on the back of the painting), they found trucks and several local television channels and quite a big crowd there, and in China when you say quite a big crowd, that can mean a very big crowd.

They went to see what was happening. Various television crews were filming a couple of pandas.

The two pandas sat tenderly embracing one another in the middle of a little island built especially for them, and from time to time they looked at the crowd staring back at them and at the cameras filming, but they didn't seem the slightest bit concerned and carried on gently licking each other's muzzles.

It was very cute, but Hector couldn't understand what all the fuss was about. Still, Vayla seemed delighted, and she sighed sweetly as she watched the pandas, probably secreting oxytocin without knowing it.

Finally, Hector found two young Chinese students who spoke English. They explained that the zookeepers had been trying for months to get the two pandas to mate. But Hi, the male panda, seemed totally uninterested in Ha, the female panda. And when she tried to attract the male's attention, he had kicked her away, so that the zookeepers had begun to wonder whether Hi wasn't a bit . . . you know what. And then two days ago Hi had suddenly become very amorous, and not only had he been intimate with Ha several times, but he kept cuddling her, when as a rule panda love was a very brief affair, after which those concerned went back to doing their own thing. And so these events were very important for the panda world, and for China, whose mascot is the panda, and even the great leaders were going to give speeches about Hi and Ha, because their new-found love was considered a good omen for the country and proof that the policies they were implementing were the right ones. And then the two students started sniggering – you could tell they were the arrogant type, probably a couple of spoilt only children.

'So, my friend, what do you make of it?'

Hector turned round; it was Professor Cormorant, of course, looking very well and accompanied by a young woman who looked like Vayla and also wore clothes from the hotel boutique. Vayla and Not gave shrieks of joy and embraced one another, after which they began a conversation punctuated with furtive giggles, while Professor Cormorant and Hector had a serious conversation. Hector noticed that the professor was leaning on a walking stick, which surprised him because he didn't recall him having a limp.

'You don't mean to tell me the pandas . . . ' said Hector.

'Of course!' said the professor. 'The same ones we took, except I modified the dose for the male.'

'How did you do it?'

'The difficulty was making sure they took it at roughly the same time. It had to land directly under their noses, and I found the way to do it,' said the professor, waving his stick and winking at Hector.

Hector understood that Professor Cormorant's bamboo cane was a blowpipe.

'And you? How is everything going with the sweet Vayla?'

Hector explained that, as the professor might imagine, everything was going very well, but even so he wanted to take the antidote.

The professor appeared surprised, but just then the two of them found themselves in front of a television camera, a microphone under their noses.

'We're from CNN,' said a young, determined-looking Asian woman. 'Would you like to say a few words about what is going on here?'

Hector saw Professor Cormorant freeze, ready to flee, then his cheeks flushed with pleasure and he declared, 'What we see here is proof that love is universal! Even among pandas! Because what is love if not a combination of affection and sexual instinct?'

At that moment, a murmur rose from the crowd because Hi was being intimate with Ha again, and she let him have his way, glancing at him sweetly over her shoulder.

Professor Cormorant was ecstatic. 'Look how happy they are, far more so than mere mating animals! They have discovered both desire and affection.'

'How interesting. And who might you be?'

'My name is Chester G. Cormorant, Ph.D., and this is my great friend Dr Hector – he's a psychiatrist. We both specialise in love.'

The young Asian woman seemed about to go into raptures – she had been looking for two English-speaking onlookers in a crowd of Chinese people, and who should she stumble upon but two experts!

'But is there some explanation as to why this is happening to these two pandas now?' she asked.

Just then, Vayla and Not came over, intrigued by the presence of the camera. They stood on either side of Hector and the professor, beaming into the lens.

'Do you know them?' asked the journalist.

'They are our research assistants,' said Professor Cormorant.

'From Benteasaryaramay University,' Hector added.

Professor Cormorant embarked on a lengthy explanation: the ingredients necessary for love were present in the brains of all mammals, a bit like musical instruments kept in a cupboard; all they needed was a conductor to make them work together.

The journalist seemed very interested, like most girls when you spoke to them about love, thought Hector.

Suddenly, he caught sight of Jean-Marcel on the other side of the crowd of Chinese people. He seemed to be looking for someone. Hector turned to Professor Cormorant to tell him but he and Not had vanished.

'A last word to sum up?' said the journalist.

'*Sabay!*' exclaimed Vayla.

Hector understood; it meant 'All is well' in Khmer. But Hector was becoming less and less sure about that.

HECTOR ISN'T THERE

THE report about Hi and Ha was shown on television channels all over the world – well, the part where they kissed each other's muzzles, not where Hi got behind Ha, because the strange thing about news programmes is that they can show you people being shot or hacked to pieces, but not two pandas making love. A few seconds of Professor Cormorant's impassioned declaration followed the panda images, and his words about love and musical instruments were repeated and translated into a lot of different languages, while next to him you could see Hector nodding in agreement, and the fresh, smiling faces of Vayla and Not.

Clara was watching CNN, as she often did to keep up her English, when she stumbled on the coverage. The first thing she noticed was how happy Hector looked. And then she thought she saw that Vayla, standing right next to him, had put her arm around his back.

Clara felt as if a jolt of electricity had passed through her body.

'What a jerk!' said Gunther.

Gunther was sitting next to her on the sofa because, there we are, sadly enough, Clara and Gunther were having an affair, and now you understand why Clara felt so sad back on the island.

You might have a low opinion of Clara – a girl sleeping with her boss in order to get promoted. Only that wasn't true at all. Clara already had a very successful career before she fell in love with Gunther so she didn't need to do that. Well, all right, you'll say, but she still fell for the alpha male – how typical. Wrong again. Clara had never been impressed by Gunther's role as the big boss, and anyway, if you think about it, Clara fell in love with Hector first, and psychiatrists are hardly ever big bosses; on the contrary, psychiatry is a profession where you don't have to obey or give orders, which was one of the things Hector liked about it, as a matter of fact.

'For Christ's sake,' said Gunther, 'he was there and they missed him by a few seconds. What's wrong? Are you crying?'

'No, I'm not,' said Clara, quickly getting up.

Clara went off to the bathroom and Gunther was upset. Because Gunther was very much in love with Clara, he wanted to start a new life with her, and, once again, he realised he still had a long way to go. He had vaguely hoped that sending Hector off on the trail of Professor Cormorant would help bring him and Clara closer, but he only had to see Clara's reaction to Hector in the company of that pretty Asian woman to realise it was not going to be easy.

In the bathroom, Clara dried her eyes and called herself a bloody fool. After all, she was the one being unfaithful to Hector – she had almost told him the truth on the island, and then she had lost her nerve – so why did she feel so bad seeing him with another woman? And given that she hadn't told him the truth because she didn't want to make him unhappy, why should she find it so unbearable to see him looking happy now?

Did this mean she still loved Hector? Or was it simply jealousy? Was jealousy a demonstration of love? Or was it that seeing those images had suddenly made her realise she was in danger of losing Hector forever? She'd known that when she started having an affair with Gunther, but, as previously mentioned, there's a big difference between knowing and feeling, and feeling is what counts most.

She had a terrible urge to speak to Hector, there and then. There was a knock on the door.

'Clara? I've made a cocktail for you.'

The big oaf, thought Clara, and at the same time she told herself she was being unfair, because she knew Gunther was crazy about her. She hadn't realised it right away, but now she was sure of it: he was completely bowled over by her. And suddenly she felt less in love with him. Oh dear, love can be so complicated, can't it!

HECTOR MEETS UP WITH A GOOD FRIEND

'THIS city is a bit crazy,' said Jean-Marcel.

He was having lunch with Hector and Vayla at the top of a tower shaped like a rocket in a revolving restaurant that turned very slowly so you could see the whole view several times over during lunch; it felt like being up in a plane or a balloon. The city stretched into the distance and everywhere skyscrapers were springing up like giant trees, and below them the river carried barges loaded with building materials, as the Chinese were putting up more and more buildings while having fewer and fewer children.

Vayla had never left her small town where the tallest building was the post office that had been built a long time ago by Hector's countrymen, and she seemed fascinated by this new city that Jean-Marcel thought was a bit crazy.

Hector was very pleased to meet up with Jean-Marcel again. Following their trip to the unsafe region and the temple recently cleared of mines, they had become real friends.

'What brings you to Shanghai?' asked Hector.

'Business, as always,' said Jean-Marcel. 'With all these towers they're building, they need signalling equipment and lots of other stuff to improve mobile telephone communication, and my company is the supplier.'

'How lucky that we bumped into each other like that,' said Hector.

'Oh, this morning the whole town was talking about those pandas – it was on all the Chinese channels – and as I had no meetings I thought I'd go and take a look. Oh man! She's got our order completely wrong!'

Hector and Jean-Marcel had asked for two beers and the waitress had brought two large tankards. Vayla frowned; she didn't like Hector drinking too much, he'd noticed, and he told himself this was a further sign of love. Vayla didn't drink alcohol because after only half a glass of wine her cheeks turned bright pink and she practically fell asleep on the spot. Hector remembered it had something to do with an enzyme deficiency common in Asian people. As a result, alcohol had a strong effect on them, but this didn't worry some of them, like the Japanese people behind them who were bravely defying their enzyme deficiency by downing tankards of beer as if it were going out of fashion.

Hector was still worrying. He hadn't been able to take the antidote yet, assuming there even was one, and he sensed that the longer he and Vayla left it, the less effect the antidote would have, because all these happy moments spent together would inevitably leave an indelible mark. Just then, Vayla smiled at him, and once again he felt waves of happiness flow through him.

'Your friend is very lovely,' said Jean-Marcel. 'Does she speak any English?'

'Not a word,' said Hector.

'And you speak no Khmer?'

'None at all.'

This reply left Jean-Marcel looking thoughtful because you can see what a relationship between a man and a woman who can't say three words to each other immediately makes you think of, and it has to be said you wouldn't be far wrong.

'And how are things between you and your wife?' asked Hector.

'Oh, not so good.'

Jean-Marcel explained they had been speaking on the phone. His wife blamed him for neglecting her over the past few years, for having been too engrossed in his job, and now it was over: she didn't love him any more. Later, she had rung Jean-Marcel back to see how he was; she was worried about how he was spending his evenings, whether he was going out with friends or staying at his hotel on his own.

'And how do you feel?' asked Hector.

'Terrible. When she says she doesn't love me any more, I feel abandoned, in a panic, and I want to see her right away. Then I feel angry with myself for neglecting her. I can't stop thinking about it. I tell myself that I've been a bit of a bastard. And then . . .'

'And then you feel angry with her because, after all, you've been a good husband to her, a good father to your children, and she's leaving you.'

Jean-Marcel looked surprised.

'Exactly! In fact, the other evening, I'd had too much to drink and I phoned her to tell her what a bitch she was, total madness. I felt pathetic, but obviously she realised I was in a bad way and I don't think she was too cross with me. And then at other times . . .'

'You tell yourself that if you separate you'll never love anyone as you've loved her. You're afraid life will be dull. Of course you'll have affairs, but nobody will make you feel like she did.'

'Good God! That's exactly it. You're very good, aren't you!'

'Oh, not really,' said Hector. 'It's just that I've been through . . .'

And it was true; before the affair with Vayla, Hector had experienced all those feelings about Clara. It was interesting to see how two men like Hector and Jean-Marcel, who weren't so alike, felt the same emotions. And, remembering some of his female patients, he said to himself that many women had been through very similar emotional upheavals. Strangely, he had the impression that none of his colleagues had ever really studied the psychology of heartache; it didn't seem a serious enough subject, yet obviously it was terribly serious, judging from the amount of suffering it caused.

Vayla touched his arm. '*Sabay*?' she asked.

'*Sabay*!' said Hector.

'*Sabay*!' said Jean-Marcel, raising his tankard, and they made a toast, smiling like happy-looking people in a Chinese beer advertisement, except that Vayla was drinking iced green tea.

HECTOR REMEMBERS

HECTOR watched Vayla as she slept. Suddenly he was reminded of these words:

Lay your sleeping head, my love,
Human on my faithless arm;
Time and fevers burn away
Individual beauty from
Thoughtful children, and the grave
Proves the child ephemeral
But in my arms till break of day
Let the living creature lie,
Mortal, guilty, but to me,
The entirely beautiful.

A poet, long ago, had experienced what Hector was feeling that night as he watched Vayla sleeping.

He remembered this poet was known to have preferred men. These verses had no doubt been written to a male companion.

Further proof that the feeling of love was universal, as Professor Cormorant would have said.

HECTOR IS NEEDY

LATER, while Vayla was watching television in her bathrobe, Hector went back to making notes, while noticing she had discovered the joys of channel-hopping. Vayla tended to stay on the music channels where very handsome young Asian men sang earnestly of their love against a background of beaches, mountains and windswept landscapes, while their sweetheart's delicate face appeared in the clouds, or else beautiful, very pale-faced Asian girls sang melancholy songs about a handsome young man with whom they couldn't get along, as shown in the flashbacks of them quarrelling and turning their backs on each other.

And yet Vayla couldn't speak Chinese or Japanese or Korean, so what she was sensitive to were not the lyrics themselves, but the pure emotions transmitted by the song's melody and by the faces, which were enough to tell that eternal tale: we love each other but we can't manage to stay together. He wrote:

> *Seedling no. 14: Women always like to dream of love even when they are already in love with someone.*

And what about men? Men could still be interested in watching porn movies even when they were in love. It was all the fault of the slightly different wiring in their brains, but this type of explanation wasn't enough to reassure women.

But it shouldn't be forgotten that men were also capable of experiencing higher emotions. Suddenly, remembering the emotions he and Jean-Marcel had felt and all the unhappy lovers he had listened to in his consulting room, Hector picked up his notebook and began writing:

The Components of Heartache

It was a rather ambitious title, but Hector told himself he was well placed to write about it since he had helped so many victims of love, men and women of all ages, who had come to sob in his consulting room.

The first component of heartache: neediness. 'I need to see him (or her), to talk to him (or her), right now.' The drug addict in need of a fix. The child separated from its mother.

This neediness was what made him and Jean-Marcel keep wanting to telephone their respective partners and stopped them concentrating on anything except the loved one. A bit like a baby screaming until its mother comes back, a built-in alarm system meant to make her come back, in fact. It was conceivable that the same areas of the brain were affected in the abandoned baby and the rejected lover. That would make an interesting research subject for Professor Cormorant, if he could be persuaded to return home, as well as to his senses. Hector felt inspired:

Of all the components, neediness is the one we experience most acutely on a physical level, not dissimilar to the withdrawal symptoms described by drug addicts deprived of their addictive substance. The area of neediness that concerns us refers to the temporary or permanent absence of the loved one whether physically or emotionally. This absence can lead to insomnia, anguish, changes in eating habits, loss of concentration – even in situations where full attention is essential (an important meeting, piloting a plane) – and on a more general level it prevents us from experiencing any pleasure, even from activities we previously considered enjoyable. These dreadful effects of neediness can be momentarily alleviated by taking a range of substances (distilled or fermented alcohols, nicotine, tranquillisers, narcotics) or even by engaging in absorbing activities (prolonged hard work, television, physical exercise, sexual relations with a new partner or with an ex-partner), but the more we push neediness away, the more violently it comes back, like a wild animal retreating only to charge with greater force.

Conversely, particular places, people and encounters that evoke memories of the loved one can intensify these attacks of neediness: the park where we walked together, the restaurant we used to meet at, the friend who witnessed our love for one another, the sweet melody the loved one enjoyed humming when he or she was feeling happy. We can experience even stronger emotions when we come across an object that the loved one has left behind. A bottle of make-up remover in the bathroom or a pair of old slippers at the back of a cupboard can move us to greater heights of suffering and emotion than any great symphony, work of art or poem.

Neediness sometimes reaches peaks of suffering the intensity of which makes us fearful of the hours to come ('How will I survive today? Tomorrow? The rest of my life?'). It also causes moments of abstraction when we are with other people, even people we like. It is generally accepted that confiding our feelings to a close friend or professional can bring real relief, although this is generally short-lived.

Vayla turned round to watch him writing, an anxious look on her face. He sensed she wanted to understand him, but Hector wouldn't have wanted to sadden or worry her with this type of reflection on love. Suddenly, thinking of the happy atmosphere that existed between him and a young woman with whom he didn't have more than a dozen words in common, Hector had another flash of inspiration:

Seedling no. 15: In love, if we really knew what the other person was saying maybe we wouldn't understand them at all.

Vayla turned back to the screen where an advert for fromage frais had just come on again, showing a choir of reindeer singing in the snow, a scene she found absolutely magical, coming as she did from a country where they didn't have snow or ice.

Hector reread his notes on the first component of heartache and found them excellent. Was this one of the effects of Professor Cormorant's drugs? Or was love such an inspiring subject? But, at the same time, his reflections weren't so encouraging: if he didn't find the antidote, and he and Vayla were separated by accident, would they each be condemned to suffer the torments of neediness for the rest of their lives?

Hector jumped; it was Vayla's voice speaking English. She was watching a pop video of Madonna who was walking down a path made of rose petals singing in English. The words were subtitled in strange spaghetti characters, probably Thai, which was close enough to Vayla's language for her to be able to understand what they meant.

Vayla repeated the English words perfectly, looking triumphantly at Hector.

CLARA STILL LOVES HECTOR

'I WANT to go to Shanghai,' said Clara.

Gunther sighed. He looked at Clara, so slight in her smart suit, and he had to remind himself that he had been a judo champion at university, had done his military service in the mountain regiment and had later restructured a whole lot of companies, at which point the business world had nicknamed him Gunther the Downsizer. He was currently head of the European and global divisions of a multinational pharmaceutical company, and here he was feeling weak and vulnerable in front of this creature named Clara who was half his size and apparently still in love with a guy who, according to what she told him, was incapable of telling a plumber what to do.

He remembered the old psychiatrist François's speech, and he told himself the man was right: they should invent a vaccine against love and to hell with Professor Cormorant and his crazy pills!

But Gunther only thought about this for three and a half seconds before managing to focus again on his goal: finding Professor Cormorant. He even said to himself that Clara's desire to go to Shanghai might help him attain it. You see, this is the strength of people like Gunther: they never confuse their emotions with their self-interest for very long, and that's why, one day, it's you who gets downsized and not them.

So, yes, why not send her to China, that diabolical little creature who brought light and darkness into his life and turned him into an unworthy husband and father.

At the same time, he knew that as soon as she had gone he would be anxious to know what she was doing every minute, but after all, thanks to the methods already being used to track Professor Cormorant and to check up on Hector, it wouldn't be so difficult to follow Clara's movements. Moreover, he could also go to China. His director of Asian operations had been asking him to come for ages; this would be an opportunity for him to go over there and tell him to pull his socks up.

'All right,' he said, 'leave whenever you want. The sooner the better.'

And he could see that Clara was a bit taken aback and that he had scored a point. Fear of rejection, he thought, it worked every time, as he knew all too well.

'You don't mind me going?' Clara asked, a little worried.

'Not in the slightest. Why should I mind?'

'Well, I don't know. Only that I'm bound to see him.'

'The way I look at it everyone has the right to experiment . . .'

'But then they have to face up to the consequences,' Clara concluded.

This was the phrase Gunther always used just before he fired someone. And he realised that a touch of anger had made him go too far and Clara might take the words he used on ordinary employees very much the wrong way.

'I'm sorry,' he said, sighing. 'Of course, I'm a bit upset that you're leaving. You know I like having you close by in the midst of all this stress. I always feel stronger when you're near me.'

And he could see Clara was full of emotion again. In fact, that was sort of how their love had begun; he had let Clara glimpse the ten per cent of him that was weak as well as the ninety per cent of him that was strong. His strength alone would never have seduced her. And yet it had seduced his previous mistresses, with whom, moreover, he had never been in love. But his admission of weakness had moved Clara, all the more so because she knew she was the only one in the company who knew about it, and then, one evening, they had found themselves kissing.

Gunther's hidden weakness was that he had a daughter who was deeply disturbed. From a young age she had started doing a lot of silly things, cutting her wrists, taking tranquillisers, associating with the wrong kind of people and worse besides. She was spending more and more time in the type of clinics rich people send their children to in Switzerland and other countries. She had already gone through quite a lot of psychiatrists for rich people, and even some psychiatrists for not so rich people on the occasions when she ended up in casualty. At one point, Gunther had thought of asking Hector to see her, but a sense of decency had held him back. His wife had also been depressed for years, and she'd been treated by various psychiatrists who didn't really believe they could cure her any more, but who helped her to stay alive.

If Hector and old François had known about his family situation, they could have had quite an interesting psychiatric discussion about it. They might have conjectured whether Gunther's wife had passed on to their daughter depressive genes which manifested themselves as borderline personality disorder. Or was it that being brought up by a depressive mother permanently disturbed the daughter? What if, on the contrary, bringing up a very difficult daughter had made the mother depressed? Perhaps it was no coincidence that the sort of strength Gunther possessed had attracted a woman with a tendency to depression who was desperately looking for someone able to protect her. Or could it be – and this question tormented Gunther – that his tendency to manipulate people, to make them do what he wanted, had disturbed both his wife and daughter? In any event, he had always sworn to himself he would never leave them, no matter how many extramarital affairs he had. And very often, after quite a gruelling day at work, he would go home to even more gruelling problems, despite always having round-the-clock support, as is often the case with rich people. But all this suffering demoralised Gunther, because he wondered about his own responsibility for his daughter's mental state and that of his wife, whom he still loved, and little by little he had opened his heart to Clara.

He would have liked to discuss all this with Hector. Did Clara love a man for his strength or for his weakness?

But, of course, it would have been difficult for the two of them to broach it because it could quickly have awakened worries of the 'Is he a better lover than me?' sort, or possibly even more precise comparisons, because, you see, men worry a lot about these kinds of things.

HECTOR AND JEALOUSY

HECTOR continued sightseeing with Vayla at Gunther's expense while waiting for a sign from Professor Cormorant. And they often met up with Jean-Marcel because you couldn't really leave a friend all on his own in a big city full of unknown Chinese people.

Well, not all of the Chinese people were unknown to Jean-Marcel; he had made a friend, Madame Li, who was his interpreter when he was doing business. Madame Li was a tall, very slim, rather bony woman. With her spectacles on, she looked a bit like a strict schoolmistress, but when she took them off, she looked much nicer, and Hector wondered whether she often took them off in front of Jean-Marcel. Li was married to a Chinese man who did a lot of business in various cities in China, and he wasn't at home very often in the evenings, a bit like Jean-Marcel. She had a little girl and a little boy, who were adorable.

One day, the four of them had dinner at a wonderful restaurant. Outside, you walked through a huge park lit by candles, a bit like Tintin's Château Moulinsart, and then you entered an enormous traditional Chinese house made entirely of wood, with several floors softly lit by lanterns so that only an occasional statue or painting stood out in the half-light. It was like being in a place of worship – the food was so good that the customers could easily have fallen to their knees in front of it. All the people having dinner looked beautiful in that light, so just imagine having dinner with Vayla and Li, who had taken her glasses off!

Hector noticed Jean-Marcel never swore in front of Li; he chose his words carefully and kept asking her if everything was to her liking. Of course, it is a good idea to be polite to your interpreter because they are very important for doing business in China.

Vayla and Li didn't speak to each other, first of all because they didn't speak the same language, but that was maybe not the only reason. Hector saw a little wrinkle of concern appear on Vayla's smooth brow each time he spoke to Li, and Li's smile froze slightly each time Vayla tried to talk a bit to Jean-Marcel, who knew a few words in Khmer. Hector could see why Vayla was worried that a more educated woman capable of communicating with Hector might be more attractive to him than a poor waitress like her, while Li must have been thinking that a woman capable of attracting Hector without even being able to talk to him might equally attract Jean-Marcel. But Vayla and Li should have realised that between true friends another man's girlfriend is like a little sister, and you wouldn't even dream of touching her, because if that isn't sacred then nothing is. Of course you can argue over the definition of a true friend and that's where the trouble starts.

And so it was Li's slightly frozen smile when she saw Vayla laughing at Jean-Marcel's grammatical mistakes in Khmer that made Hector realise that even if nothing had happened yet, Li and Jean-Marcel could be about to become more closely linked. And it became even clearer to him why Vayla liked the subtitled pop videos on the Asian music channels so much – she no longer wanted to be the only one who couldn't talk to him.

It was another confirmation for Hector that with love comes jealousy. But what sort of love?

Professor Cormorant had mentioned two components of love: sexual desire and attachment. Hector apologised and took out his little notebook again.

Seedling no. 16: Jealousy is inseparable from desire.

And yet he remembered the shed with the young girls in Vayla's country. The men who went there desired those young girls, but not one of them was jealous of the girls seeing several clients before or after him.

But Hector imagined settling in that town and going every day to the shed (his life is a mess, Clara has left him and so has Vayla, his patients have committed suicide, his parents are dead, he has received a huge tax reminder, grown very fat and his hair is falling out). He told himself he would probably end up preferring one of the young women to all the others, he would become attached to her and then no longer be able to tolerate the thought of her seeing other clients, to the point where he would be prepared to arrange things with the *mama-san* (the person in charge of human resources, in several different Asian languages) and the *mama-san*'s friends so that the young woman could give up that unhappy profession. And Hector was even more convinced things would take this course because something similar had happened to him during his first trip to China, the slight difference being that he had become attached to the young woman before realising what her unhappy profession was.

And so he wrote:

Seedling no. 17: Jealousy is a sign of attachment.

But that wasn't right either. He had known couples who no longer desired one another but who still felt a strong bond and in those cases the one didn't feel jealous when the other got laid – as Jean-Marcel put it. On the other hand, Hector remembered men who felt almost no affection for their wives, but who were driven crazy by the thought of her having a brief encounter with another man. So did that count as love? Maybe there were two types of jealousy: feeling jealous of the other desiring another, or feeling jealous of the other possibly becoming attached to another. Maybe there were as many components to jealousy as there were to love.

And maybe . . . Hector had a sudden eureka moment. Love must contain as many components as heartache!

'*Sabay!*' he cried.

'*Sabay!*' declared Vayla, overjoyed to see Hector so happy.

Jean-Marcel explained to Li what the Khmer word meant, and Li thought about it and said that in Shanghai Chinese you could have said '*Don Ting Hao De*'.

And they all said '*Don Ting Hao De*' and Hector said to himself that this was another moment of happiness. But moments are fleeting things.

CLARA IS SAD

On the plane, Clara thought sadly about what had prompted her to love Hector less. As she was a methodical girl who was used to breaking things down into their constituent parts, she took a notebook from her bag, and felt a slight pang because it was a notebook she had taken from Hector, who bought them in packets of ten.

Why has our love faded?

Because I am angry with him for not having married me when I wanted?

There was some truth in this: at the beginning of their relationship, Clara was very much in love; so was Hector, but he felt in no hurry to get married, that is, to commit. Hearing his parents say what a crucial thing marriage was and how terribly important it was to choose a wife well because, as far as disasters were concerned, divorce came third after nuclear war and the bubonic plague, Hector had grown a little apprehensive about marriage and its air of permanence. As a result he had disregarded Clara's eagerness to marry, and now she was the one who no longer wanted to commit. At the same time, Clara didn't hold his past failings against him, because she knew about life and, anyway, when you don't want to marry someone any more, it is difficult to be upset with them for not having wanted to marry you in the past. But perhaps she was a little angry with him all the same for having spoilt the freshness and spontaneity of her love for him.

Because time destroys everything in the long run and we have known each other too long?

Because he no longer holds any mystery for me?

The answers to these questions were all more or less the same. Clara knew Hector inside out, his good sides and his not so good sides, so it was true he no longer really held any mystery for her.

Because his profession makes him less fun and less energetic?

If this was true, it was very unfair, she thought, but who said love was fair? Hector's profession often made him very tired, and when he got home he was unable to speak for an hour at least, even when they were both invited out to dinner in town. Some evenings Hector would drink too many aperitifs in order to put himself in the mood and sometimes he would say silly things that irritated Clara. On holiday or at weekends, Clara liked to be active, to do sports, but Hector said he was too tired for that and he spent his time snoozing, relaxing or sleeping, and also making love, but mostly he spent his weekends lying on his back, and this also irritated Clara.

Because I was attracted to Gunther right from the beginning?

Clara chewed her pen. This was a difficult thing to admit. What if it were the main reason? She loved Hector but Gunther had come along, and she had been attracted to the man, his energy, his intellect (which, let's be clear, was simply different from that of Hector, who wasn't stupid either), his swift decision making (very different from Hector in this regard, admittedly), his ability to switch very quickly from crude anger to polite composure (Hector never lost his temper) and his gift for seeing the bigger picture from a strategic point of view whilst being able to pay great attention to detail (Hector wouldn't have made a bad strategist, but detail bored him).

What really upset Clara was that this affair was a cliché: the girl who falls for her boss, like the student falling for her teacher, and Clara couldn't stand the idea of being a cliché. For her it was demeaning.

She preferred to tell herself she had fallen in love with Gunther because she had been moved when he began confiding in her about the hellishness of his home life with his wife and daughter.

And it was true. The intimacy that had grown up between them as a result of these confidences had blossomed into love. (Hector had in fact already explained this to her: intimacy can lead to a woman loving a man she is not even initially attracted to, and psychiatrists have to be careful about this type of love in female patients with whom they develop a close relationship.) But let's imagine it was her colleague Lemercier from research and development, who liked hiking in the Vesoul region, around his parents' pretty converted farmhouse; yes, what if it was that nice boy who had begun telling her about some similar family problems, would she have been as moved?

This was the sort of question Clara didn't really like to dwell on, all the more so because in her youth she had been a left-wing activist, and so the idea of falling in love with a man known as Gunther the Downsizer upset her three times as much.

The plane arrived over Shanghai during the day, and the city was a forest of skyscrapers rising from the earth in the misty daylight. An enchanted concrete forest, thought Clara, who had a way with words.

This was just as well because now she had to come up with some damn good ones to inform Hector that she no longer loved him and that she was having an affair with a man she did love, Gunther, her boss. On second thoughts, perhaps she shouldn't tell him the last part, because it might make Hector less inclined to find Professor Cormorant, and at least that mission kept his mind off things.

Why then had Gunther allowed her to go to Shanghai in order to tell Hector their relationship was over? Because he trusts me, she thought. Which proves that when a thought reassures you it can prevent you from thinking any further.

And what if Hector had fallen deeply in love with that young Asian girl she had glimpsed on television? What a cliché! Clara thought again with a shudder. The Western man, no longer exactly young, falls into the arms of a sweet young Asian girl who smiles at him all the time. Very nice, really, well done, Dr Hector!

She recalled an expression her parents often used when her two equally insufferable little brothers came telling tales: 'The pot calling the kettle black'. The same could be said of her and Hector in this situation, she thought to herself, and of men and women in general when it came to love.

A long way below her, Hector and Vayla were engaged in doing just that – making love, that is. They hadn't had time to see themselves on television. But Vayla had watched enough to be able to sing later in Hector's ear: '"I just can't get you out of my head . . ."'

HECTOR'S LIFE IS COMPLICATED

Dear friend,

We haven't seen each other now for nearly three weeks. Forgive my sudden disappearance, but I realised that our presence next to the two excited pandas would very quickly attract the attention of the people who are looking for me, and so, as Napoleon once said about love, the only safety was in flight.

I intend to stay in the area for the time being, so expect a sign from me. I have found two extremely talented chemists here who are willing to take part in my experiments. This country is a veritable powerhouse of creativity, intelligence and youth.

Having seen the charming Vayla, I encourage you not even to entertain the thought of leaving her. She has a smile of real happiness and, as you know from reading my latest research, that means she has a gift for remaining happy in the face of life's vagaries. Do you know how much a good-natured woman is worth, my young friend? She is priceless, I tell you. My Not has her attractions, but in that way she is a more tormented soul, which isn't surprising when you know what she went through as a child – I'll tell you about it one day.

I must leave you now because my young collaborator has just come to tell me we are about to finish a new experiment.

Sabay!

By the way, did you know that expression comes from another, which means to eat rice, meaning when we eat rice all is well? The simple happiness of these people is moving when you think about what happened to them after we introduced them, one after the other, to those two Western inventions, Marxism gone mad and the B52 bomber.

Chester G. Cormorant

This message made Hector feel deeply uneasy. Professor Cormorant was carrying on with his experiments. And yet he remembered that his first chemist had been committed after trying out one of his new drugs. What he said about Vayla also alarmed him: he knew Professor Cormorant was an expert in deciphering people's facial expressions and emotions and that his studies had allowed him to identify the type of smile which could predict whether a person was predisposed towards happiness. But this would make it even harder for him to leave Vayla, assuming he was able to at all. And, in addition, the professor had said nothing more about an antidote.

He watched Vayla sleeping peacefully, oblivious to his crises of conscience, her graceful profile silhouetted against the pillow. All at once she must have felt him looking at her, because she opened her eyes and gave him a big smile. Hector was filled with tenderness towards her. His brain was secreting oxytocin, Professor Cormorant would have said.

But why leave Vayla? you may ask. If Hector and Vayla were happy together, why not get married? Yes, you've guessed, it was because Hector was still in love with Clara. And, as a matter of fact, when he looked at the computer again, he noticed a new email in his inbox. Vayla had got up and was sitting in front of the television.

Dear Hector,
I'm coming to Shanghai. I'll be at the Peace Hotel tonight. Where are you?
Love Clara

Hector became intensely agitated. He replied:

Dear Clara,
I'm at . . .

No. He pressed delete.

Dear Clara,
I can meet you at your hotel.

No. He pressed delete.

Dear Clara,
Let me know when you arrive. Here is my Chinese mobile number.

He had bought a Chinese pre-pay mobile so he could communicate more secretly with Professor Cormorant, although the professor had explained to him that Gunther's company had enough money and contacts to employ a few people from the Chinese secret services who would be only too happy to do some overtime in order to have some jam on their bread, or in this case, some lacquer on their duck. And Hector's new number would be discovered and tapped within twenty-four hours. But that didn't matter, because Gunther must have known Clara was coming to Shanghai.

Vayla cried out in front of the television. Hector looked at the screen.

You could see Professor Cormorant giving his impassioned speech about love next to the panda enclosure, Hector standing beside him and Vayla's smile lighting up the whole screen. Hector's face began to flush; now he knew why Clara was coming to Shanghai!

Vayla threw her arms round his neck and covered him with kisses. He realised that, for her, seeing them together on television was like a blessing, an amazing miracle that had happened to her, a poor waitress. It was just like one of the fairy tales from her country, where the benevolence of the gods suddenly shines down on a simple peasant walking barefoot beside a paddy field.

HECTOR IS CROSS WITH HIMSELF

Hector woke up. Vayla was sleeping soundly next to him rolled up in the bedspread with only her pretty nose poking out, because, for her, air conditioning was like winter in the mountains.

Hector began thinking about Clara again.

She was about to arrive in Shanghai, so what was he to do?

Introduce her to Vayla and ask them to be friends? No, psychiatrists are said to be a bit mad sometimes but not to that extent. Hector told himself that, in an ideal world, he would have liked to pursue his love for Vayla without losing Clara. Even Professor Cormorant's drug hadn't destroyed the bond between them, which he could still feel was very strong.

So why had she begun not to love him any more?

Hector started thinking.

The Second Component of Heartache

The second component of what is commonly referred to as heartache is guilt. We blame ourselves for the loss of the loved one, and regret everything we did and said that might have contributed to the waning of love. Especially painful are memories of our insensitivity, neglect or even unkindness towards the loved one, who seems to us with hindsight to have been remarkably generous in loving us despite our shortcomings. This self-criticism invariably takes the form of questions we put to ourselves: 'How could I have been so neglectful when he (or she) needed my help? How could I have been so irritable with him (or her) when all they were doing was trying to put me in a good mood? Why did I stupidly flirt with someone else when I knew it would make them suffer? Why did I let that idiot chase them without doing anything, as though I were so sure of myself or, on the contrary, so unsure? How could I have refused to respond to their references to our future together when at the time that was what they were dreaming of and all they wanted was to love me?'

He kept remembering all the times he hadn't been very nice to Clara, and when he had made her cry, at the beginning of their relationship, when he had calmly explained to her that he wasn't sure he wanted to commit to their relationship, or when he had been in a bad mood and snapped at her. All those occasions when Clara had been in tears, or had looked sad after suffering rejection, indifference or criticism from him, all those occasions came back to him. He felt like shouting at himself, although he wouldn't have gone so far as to call himself a bit of a bastard like Jean-Marcel.

During these reminiscences, the loved one appears as a shining example of tenderness, honesty and generosity towards us, while we reveal ourselves to be neglectful, selfish and indifferent to our lover's happiness. These guilt-ridden thoughts can prompt us to write long letters full of remorse and promises of our undying love to the loved one. Writing these letters brings us great comfort, but it is brief, all the more so because the loved one doesn't usually reply.

Clara had not replied to his first desperate emails. And yet here she was on her way to Shanghai in person.

Vayla opened one eye and began smiling as soon as she saw him, then suddenly gave him a concerned, questioning look. She had sensed Hector was worried. Hector returned her smile and wrote:

Seedling no. 18: Love means sensing immediately when the other is unhappy.

HECTOR MAKES AN IMPORTANT DISCOVERY

Hector had fallen asleep. And when he woke up Vayla had gone. This made him uneasy. How would she manage all alone in this city where the names of the streets were in Chinese, and where the taxi drivers never understood the way you pronounced an address? As a result, they often took you to the wrong place altogether! That meant that unless you kept the business card of your hotel with you, you were liable to find yourself eating reheated noodles under a flyover several days later.

In the hotel lobby, Hector found Jean-Marcel sitting near the bar, not looking very happy.

'Are you all right?' Hector asked.

'Oh, the same old story. I keep blaming myself for things. No doubt you've heard it all before.'

'That's for sure! You haven't seen Vayla, have you?'

'Yes, I just saw her walk past. In fact, she looked like she was in a hurry.'

'I wonder where she went. What if she gets lost?'

'Oh, don't worry, you can't get lost here – someone will always find you. And, anyway, I don't see a girl like her letting go of a guy like you.'

'What do you mean?' asked Hector, wondering whether Jean-Marcel's remark was as complimentary as all that.

'Imagine her life back there. And she's one of the relatively privileged ones. Supporting her whole family on her salary, liable to be laid off as soon as there are no guests, being propositioned by losers – not you, I know it's not like that – and, what's more, if she was working at that hotel it is precisely because she didn't want to be a so-called *massage-madame*, but that could still be her fate if things turn out badly. The other alternative is to marry a man from her country. Of course, there are exceptions, but, believe me, they are real machos, the kind that died out a long time ago back home. That's why, in my opinion, even left in the middle of a snow storm without a compass, she would find you.'

But then, Hector wondered, was Vayla attracted to him out of self-interest or out of love? Of course, he could assume it was love because she had taken one of Professor Cormorant's drugs. And her face showed every sign of love when she woke up and saw him. But let us imagine their relationship had taken the same turn without any drugs? How could he tell if Vayla stayed with him out of love or out of self-interest? In fact, all men who had a higher social status than their wives could ask themselves the same question (or not).

And what about him? Did he love Vayla or was he just attracted by her beauty and the sexual harmony they enjoyed? This was a question all beautiful women could ask themselves: did men love them for who they were, or for their attractiveness, for the erotic stimulation they produced, and also for the prestige men gained from showing them off, impressing the crowd with a beautiful trophy wife? The same question also applied, to a lesser extent, to rich women and handsome men.

Hector wrote in his notebook:

Seedling no. 19: Could love be a combination of self-interest and emotions?

Again, it was complicated, because there was material self-interest, which was generally considered very different from love, but also emotional self-interest, which was generally considered the same as love. A woman could fall in love with a man who had more money, not for the money in itself, but because she felt protected and reassured, and that feeling of security was what made her love thrive. And her love might endure even if the man lost all his money – or not, and that would be the real test. She might also fall for a man who was successful in his field not because she particularly liked successful men but because of the energy and determination that had allowed him to attain his position.

We fall in love with someone who is beautiful because beauty creates desire and at the same time it gives us a feeling of peace and contentment, which is part of the sentiment we describe as love. 'Beauty is a promise of happiness,' a great writer from Hector's country had once said, a man who himself was not very handsome and rather unhappy in love.

But of course the ideal would be to love somebody in spite of their imperfections and faults, whatever happens.

You should be able to perceive the beauty of the loved one in all its splendour, even if everyone else is blind to it. He had to write that down:

Seedling no. 20: Love means still seeing the other's beauty when nobody else does any more.

Hector began to sing:

'Pushed aside by younger, stronger arms than mine,
Will you love me still when part of me has died . . .'

'A charming song,' said Jean-Marcel. 'Only it's the kind of question it's best not to ask yourself.'

'I was just wondering about the difference between love and self-interest. What do you think?'

'Well, my friend, twenty years in Asia has given me plenty of time for reflection. I've seen it all, believe me, and here, of course, a white man is nearly always rich by comparison. And there are a lot of young people in these countries, and therefore a lot of young women, and it makes some men lose the plot.'

'So what?'

'So I've seen it all – for instance the romantic types, who married bar hostesses; you know, the saviour complex: "She's too good for that; she's different from the others." Everyone was afraid for those men, and they were right to be – mostly the men got taken to the cleaners, and occasionally even thrown out of the country when the sisters had connections. But in some cases, even when the men became penniless and old, the girls stayed with them, caring for them and supporting them, sometimes until their dying day. Out of love or duty? I don't know. But in any case there was some bond that wasn't self-interest. And then there were a few happy couples in the bunch, excellent wives and mothers, who, frankly, to begin with, you would never have believed had it in them. The fact is, in poor countries, completely normal girls find themselves making a living from their physical attributes, and often it's to feed their little brothers and sisters who are still living in the countryside. And, you know, I've seen some of the messiest situations involving wives from the most sophisticated families.'

'So it's hard to differentiate between love and self-interest.'

'When everything's going well, it's very hard to tell; the real test is when things go wrong, like in your song. You know what they say during the marriage ceremony, what they used to say anyway: "For better, for worse, for richer, for poorer, in sickness and in health . . ."'

Jean-Marcel sometimes seemed a bit rough and ready, but you could see he had the ability to think about things, especially when he was feeling a bit down.

Hector wrote in his notebook:

Seedling no. 21: Love proves itself when put to the test.

Suddenly he noticed Vayla entering the lobby. The moment she saw Hector her face lit up.

Hector had time to write:

Seedling no. 22: Love is, smiling the moment you see one another.

HECTOR'S LIFE IS COMPLICATED

AFTER a shower and a change of clothes, Clara felt as good as new as she made her way to the lobby of the Peace Hotel. It looked like the inside of a castle with its bare stone walls, stained-glass windows and old-fashioned furniture, except that it was invaded by a steady flow of businessmen and tourists from all over the world, including Chinese tourists, because China is as big as several countries put together.

All of a sudden she felt discouraged. What had she come to Shanghai for? To see Hector of course, but what for?

To tell him that she didn't love him any more? She knew that wasn't entirely true, otherwise she wouldn't be there. To tell him she still loved him? But in that case how could she explain her affair with Gunther? And, anyway, she loved Gunther, she knew that, with a love that was more passionate and more overwhelming, different from the more serene but perhaps deeper love she felt for Hector. She ordered some mineral water, thinking to herself that, in an ideal world, she would have liked to pursue her love for Gunther while knowing that Hector was still bound to her. *That means I'm no better than a man who wants to have a mistress and keep his wife*. She also realised that it had been the sight of the pretty Asian girl that had sparked off her fear of losing Hector forever, which she wasn't exactly proud of.

Still, she might as well be clear in her mind about it. She called Hector.

It was a bad moment because Hector had gone back up to the hotel room with Vayla and, surprise surprise, Vayla had given him a note from Professor Cormorant.

'Not,' explained Vayla, and Hector understood that two young Khmer women let loose in a foreign city can always find each other when necessary.

Dear friend,

Let us once more stray from the common pathways of the internet, spied upon by petty souls, and communicate via winged messengers like those that served the gods. And, by the way, do they not resemble goddesses, our two lovely apsaras*? Come this instant and meet me at my laboratory, where you will witness science in the making. Leave the charming Vayla behind to do some shopping on your expense account – because, believe me, knowing what you know, they won't dare refuse you anything – and go to the corner of Fuxing Dong Lu and Wan Bang Zhong Lu. Pretend to be interested in the paintings – a fine collection of Chinese modern art, by the way – go into the gallery, ask where the toilets are and, once you reach the end of the* *corridor, hurry through the second door on the right. One last but important detail: make sure you open the door at exactly 12.45. If it doesn't open, come back and follow the same procedure exactly one hour later.*

In anticipation of our summit meeting, which I am already looking forward to,

Yours,
Chester the Brilliant

Just then, Hector's phone rang, and it was Clara.

'Well, I'm here. Where are you?'

'Er . . .'

'Are you at your hotel?'

'Yes, but I'm about to go out.'

'Do you want to meet somewhere else?'

Hector looked at his watch. It was 12.18; if he met Clara now, he would be unable to keep to Professor Cormorant's schedule.

He explained to Clara that he had to leave his hotel right away for an important meeting.

'Who with? Cormorant?'

'No, no.'

'With that girl.'

'No . . .'

'Listen, call me as soon as you're done.'

'I will.'

As he rang off, he saw Vayla's pretty brow knitted in a frown: she had understood that Hector had been speaking to a woman who was causing him problems.

'*Sabay!*' he said, but he could see this didn't calm her.

She shot him a reproachful look.

'*Noblem!*' he added, kissing her, because this was another one of the few expressions he shared with Vayla: it was how she had understood and remembered 'no problem'. This time, she smiled and Hector left with a light heart, more or less.

HECTOR GOES FOR A DRIVE

THE gallery was in a big street lined with beautiful old brick buildings, which looked like the ones you find in New York. This wasn't surprising, seeing as they dated from the same time and could well have been designed by the same architects who were in fashion back then.

Hector found the painter's work very interesting: a lot of the canvases showed young Chinese women against a background of factories, ploughed fields or construction sites, a bit like propaganda posters, but you could see the artist's intention was to make fun of propaganda, because the young girls didn't really look as if they were thinking about building the future of socialism. If anything, they looked bored, or as if they'd rather be having fun or texting their boyfriends on their mobiles.

The young Chinese woman who ran the gallery – one of the artist's models? – gave him a charming greeting and Hector was sorry to disappoint her since he wasn't going to buy anything, not this time anyway. He walked towards the toilets, checking his watch: it was 12.44. He paused in front of the second door on the right and opened it.

He found himself in a small side street behind the building and was nearly run over by a big black car with tinted windows, which pulled up right in front of him.

'Come on, get in!' said Professor Cormorant.

Hector found himself sitting beside the professor as the car sped off, chauffeured by a woman who, to Hector's surprise, was wearing the uniform of the Chinese army.

'Allow me to present Captain Lin Zaou, from the People's Liberation Army. She's a very good driver and, even better, she's the reason we're never stopped by the police.'

The chauffeur turned round for a moment to greet him, and Hector saw a very stern-faced Chinese woman in an army cap and a collar studded with gold stars.

Professor Cormorant had apparently made a lot of connections in Shanghai. The Chinese have a word for it: *guanxi*, and without *guanxi* you won't get far in China.

'What's good,' said Professor Cormorant, 'is to see that people with ideals are interested in my research.'

'Where are we going?'

'To my new laboratory!'

The car drove up an access ramp and they found themselves on a flyover. They sailed past a lot of very tall skyscrapers, so many that Hector couldn't see the ones he had noticed when he arrived and used to get his bearings. Back in his own country, Hector lived in a big city, but now he realised it wasn't that big after all.

'Professor Cormorant, before we do anything else, I need the antidote. I don't want to be tied to Vayla forever.'

'But why not, young man?'

'Because . . .'

It was difficult to explain. First of all because Hector was still in love with Clara, and he didn't think either

Clara or Vayla would want to share him. (Mind you, this solution might have suited Hector quite well, because with men it's often like that; they don't necessarily like cut-and-dried solutions in love; they want to be nice to everyone, but there's always one woman who wants them only to be nice to her and not to others.) But also the idea that his and Vayla's love was the result of a drug bothered him: Hector felt that it was an infringement of their liberty, and possibly of their human dignity, although that was very difficult to explain to Professor Cormorant, who seemed so pleased with his experiments.

'Don't worry, you will get it,' said Professor Cormorant, 'but I still think it will make you unhappy, or rather that you will be throwing away an opportunity to be immensely happy.'

Hector decided not to press the point – all he wanted was the professor's word that there was an antidote. He decided to ask him about love, as he knew the professor liked talking about that.

'The other day I wrote: *Could love be a combination of self-interest and emotions?* I asked myself whether self-interest doesn't lead to emotion – a woman wants a man's status because it offers her security, but ends up falling head over heels in love with him – and, equally, whether our emotions don't serve our self-interest – a man feels he is in love with a pretty woman, but deep down having that pretty face near him will help confirm his social status in the eyes of the world.'

'Excellent!' roared Professor Cormorant. 'But you have only spoken about one component of love. Two at the most. And you are speaking of attraction rather than love.'

Hector was pleased: in only a few words Professor Cormorant had given him a foretaste of everything interesting he had to say about love. But, just then, the Chinese chauffeur in the army cap informed them in English that they were being followed.

They saw a big German car behind them, or rather behind the car that was behind them, because the driver must be clever, but not as clever as Captain Lin Zaou of the People's Liberation Army.

'For God's sake!' said Professor Cormorant. 'You were followed!'

'Or perhaps you were,' said Hector.

'Impossible!'

They might have gone on arguing about it, but their car swerved abruptly towards an exit, so fast it felt like it was falling, and for the next five minutes all Hector and Professor Cormorant could do was hold on to the door handles, amid a screeching of tyres. Then the car slowed down.

'We've lost them,' said the captain.

Hector and Professor Cormorant sat up straight.

They were now driving along a narrow street lined with plane trees and cottages – you'd have thought you were in Hector's country, which was understandable, because a long time ago that part of town had belonged to his country. The car drove through a gateway and parked in a courtyard with two plane trees and what must once have been stables running along one side. At the foot of one of the trees, Hector noticed a shrine with fruit and sticks of incense placed in front of a statue of Buddha. A pair of French windows opened and Not appeared, smiling, followed by two young, effeminate Chinese men.

'My assistants,' exclaimed Professor Cormorant.

The two young Chinese men greeted Hector. One of them had very untidy hair that stood up on end as though he had just got out of bed, except that it was done on purpose, and the other was wearing purple glasses and an earring.

'Nice to meet you. Professor Cormorant very good,' they said to Hector in English.

'Never mind the compliments,' said Chester, 'let's take you straight to the lab,' and Hector knew he wasn't going to be bored.

CLARA MEETS VAYLA

ANOTHER person who wasn't bored was Clara, who had gone directly to Hector's hotel. She was perfectly aware of its name, since Gunther had given it to her.

Clara was in the lobby, which looked like an Indian palace, with lots of comfortable settees, which were so pretty that the thought occurred to Clara that one of them would look good in Hector's consulting room, before she realised how inappropriate that thought was. She decided to sit on one of these splendid couches while she waited for Hector to come back.

Of course, this was what Clara told herself, that she had come here to wait for Hector, but it would have been much easier to ring him and arrange a meeting. In fact, Clara had only one thought in her head: to catch sight of the pretty Asian girl she had seen at Hector's side.

She began to watch people coming and going, and what with the businessmen and -women assembled at one of the lobby bars before going off to a meeting, the tourist couples arriving exhausted from their morning excursions and the hotel staff dressed in their white, faintly Indian-looking uniforms, it made for quite a crowd, and suddenly, coming out of the arcade of boutiques, she saw the charming young Asian girl. Clara had to admit it: she really was lovely.

Vayla was carrying rather a lot of bags with the names of the various boutiques on them, and Clara felt a little pang as she wondered whether all this expenditure was a gift from Hector or whether it was being paid for by the company, in which case Gunther, in a sort of poetic justice, was footing the bill for Hector's new lover's purchases.

Vayla felt a bit tired after all that shopping, and so she sat down with a graceful little movement in one of the armchairs in the lobby, a few yards away from Clara, who was still watching her.

Clara looked for any defects, but because she was essentially honest, she recognised that there weren't many to find.

A waiter approached Vayla with a menu and asked her what she would like. She looked embarrassed. The waiter spoke in English then Chinese then English again, but Vayla still had the embarrassed look of someone who is afraid of making a blunder. Finally, she asked for an orange juice in the voice of someone who has learnt the words off by heart. The waiter went away and Clara began to fret.

The girl didn't speak English, and as it was unlikely she spoke Hector's language, and he didn't know any Asian languages, this provided an insight into their relationship which worried Clara. She tried to say to herself: So that explains it, she's just a bed friend; his lordship is enjoying himself with a woman who isn't capable of answering back. At the same time, she knew Hector and realised it couldn't be true; it wasn't his style to make love several times without becoming involved. He must be attached to this girl in a way that wasn't just physical. Perhaps he wanted to help her, to protect her, to take her away from the place where he had found her? Clara realised it was this thought that caused her the most pain. Hector having a passionate liaison with a pretty local girl wasn't exactly pleasant, but the idea that he could be attached to her for other reasons, and above all because he wanted to take care of her, was absolutely unbearable.

And what about you, missy, with your Gunther, are you in any position to criticise? Of course not. Life really was very complicated. Clara suddenly felt overwhelmed by the vastness of the lobby, by all these people coming and going, and by the presence right next to her of Vayla ensconced in her enormous armchair, like a precious jewel nestling in its case.

Just then, Vayla sensed she was being watched and glanced at Clara.

When you come from a country like Vayla's you learn early on to read people, to sense who will be kind to you and who won't, because, in countries like that, a child's life is quite precarious.

She saw a Western woman, quite pretty, older than her, but still young, gazing at her with surprising intensity.

Vayla felt uneasy because she had the impression Clara was a nice person and at the same time she sensed waves of hostility radiating towards her. She felt dazed for a moment, leaving the waiter to put a large glass of orange juice full of sparkling ice cubes down in front of her, and then all of a sudden the only possible explanation dawned on her, as clear as day.

'Darling Hector?' This was the expression Vayla had used in order to ask Hector if there was another woman in his life in his faraway country. And from the awkward way he had said '*sort of*', she had understood that even if only '*sort of*' there was another woman in his life and he loved her.

She started feeling afraid. How could she hope to compete with this woman whose skin was so pale – a sure sign of refinement and beauty – who knew about a whole world of which she was ignorant, who could no doubt drive and use a computer, and who knew Hector much better than she did? Vayla knew Hector found her pretty, but that must be because he had forgotten his partner's milky-white complexion. Confronted with such a powerful rival, even Professor Cormorant's love potion would be useless.

Vayla began to resign herself to defeat. It was her destiny to have met Hector, her incredible good luck. And it was her destiny to have him taken away from her again. A tear dropped into her orange juice.

HECTOR DOES SOME SCIENCE

In a huge Plexiglas cage, dozens of little mice were copulating furiously. They looked like some sort of vibrating fur carpet.

'Look,' said Professor Cormorant, 'they've been given compound A. Lots of sexual desire. I put a bit too much in my first concoction.'

Hector remembered what the hotel manager had said about the professor's tendency to chase after the female staff at the hotel.

In another cage, a couple of mandarin ducks were lovingly rubbing their beaks together.

'Compound B. Affection. Oxytocin – slightly modified of course,' the professor added, winking.

The ducks were a touching sight and, with their crests and multicoloured plumage, they reminded Hector of characters in an opera declaring their love.

'The problem is they're so keen on canoodling it stops them eating. Too strong a dose at the beginning, or perhaps the formula's still not quite right.'

'But won't it kill them if they don't eat?'

'*Of loving at will, of loving to death, in the land that is like you* . . . Actually, we're obliged to separate them from time to time, and we take the opportunity to force-feed them.'

'Force-feed them?'

'Have you ever eaten mandarin duck pâté?' the professor asked, and immediately burst out laughing, as did the two young Chinese men, for this was clearly one of their favourite jokes.

'Professor Cormorant very funny!' said Lu, the one with the ruffled hair.

'Very very funny!' added Wee, the one with the purple-tinted glasses.

And their laughter echoed under the vaulted brick ceiling. The laboratory had been set up in a series of cellars belonging to a former wine merchant from the time of the International Settlement, who had made his deliveries to his customers by horse-drawn cart, hence the old stables in the courtyard.

Hector had noticed numerous new-fangled-looking machines, some with flat screens where you could see spinning molecules, computers unlike any you might have at home, and a nuclear magnetic resonance imaging machine like the one he had seen at Professor Cormorant's university, and of course an animal house, containing different species, which stared at you mournfully from their Plexiglas cages. It all looked like it had been set up very recently, and since Gunther had blocked all Professor Cormorant's accounts Hector wondered where he had found the money for it all. Who was paying the young Chinese men and women working in one of the rooms in front of their flat screens?

'Our biggest problem is estimating how long the effects will last. In humans, it is difficult to differentiate between a lasting effect of the product and a lasting effect of the early stages of the love experience. Not and I, for example: do we continue to love each other because the initial dose is still active in our brains or because we've got used to such an amazing degree of harmony that now it's become a habit?'

'And how can you find out?'

'By studying the effects on animals that have no emotional memory. I'll show you a pair of rabbits in a minute . . .'

'But does it really matter either way?' asked Hector. 'The end result is the same, whether it's an effect of the product or an effect of learning together: a love that lasts.'

'How can you be sure it will last? After all, our recent relationships, yours and mine, are only a few weeks old . . .'

Hector saw a glimmer of hope – maybe the effects of the drug would wear off.

'. . . but I can also tell you that six months ago, at the university, I made two ducks fall in love, just like the ones you saw, and the faculty have written to inform me that the little darlings still love each other tenderly! And, what's more, that drug hadn't been perfected!'

Hector's hopes were instantly dashed. He and Vayla would be together indefinitely. The professor's roguish expression, like an overgrown child pleased at having played a clever prank, suddenly made him angry.

'But, Professor Cormorant, we aren't ducks! And what about freedom of choice?'

'Hang on, people will always be free to—'

'Love isn't simply a question of drugs! What about commitment? And compassion? We aren't rabbits, and we aren't pandas!'

'For heaven's sake, calm down, everything's fine!'

'You can't play around with love! Love is a serious matter!'

'Indeed, and we take it very seriously, Dr Hector.'

It was a tall Chinese man in a suit who had spoken. He had come in noiselessly and was watching them with a smile, flanked by Lu and Wee. He looked older than Hector, but younger than the professor, and he had intelligent eyes behind his fine titanium glasses, and a smile like a film star's. His suit was so immaculate you wondered if he would dare sit down in it, but he had the look of a man who was in the habit of daring when he judged it necessary.

'Dr Wei,' said Professor Cormorant, 'the one sponsoring all this research!'

'I am only a humble intermediary,' said Dr Wei, narrowing his intelligent eyes.

HECTOR HAS A SHOCK

HECTOR returned to his hotel, all alone in the back of the big car driven by Captain Lin Zaou. He watched the amazing Shanghai skyscrapers glide by in the hazy late-afternoon light, but he didn't care about them. He was very worried by the association between Professor Cormorant and Dr Wei.

'We see love as a cause of social chaos,' Dr Wei had said. 'Instead of starting families or helping the economy to thrive, young people waste their energy flitting from one person to the other, a hedonistic, selfish pursuit. Or else they suffer from heartache, and as a result some of our most brilliant students miss the opportunity to attend the best universities, throwing away their futures and their contribution to their country. And those who do marry in accordance with their parents' wishes (as always used to be the custom until recent times) mope about, particularly the girls, it has to be said, wondering if it is right to stay with a man they don't feel sufficiently in love with! And all this, of course, is the fault of the media, turning their heads with all their talk of love!'

Hector was sure that this sort of torment had existed long before the media came along, and that you could find lots of Chinese poems dating back centuries about women weeping because their husbands were unkind, and grieving for their first loves. However, he didn't say anything because he wanted to hear the whole of Dr Wei's argument, and Dr Wei was obviously a man who was used to talking for a long time without being interrupted.

As if to demonstrate this, Lu and Wee were listening to him with an air of great respect, giving little nods of agreement. And yet Hector had the impression they were only pretending; there was something strange but he couldn't put his finger on it. The only enjoyable thing about the situation was imagining Gunther's face when he discovered that the vast Chinese market had just slipped through his fingers. Should Hector send him a report informing him of this catastrophe?

The car dropped him in front of his hotel, and suddenly he remembered another problem he had to deal with, one that was as complicated as the future of China and Taiwan: Vayla and Clara.

He felt rather depressed and wondered whether it might not be a side effect of the drug. He was about to go through the revolving door when he bumped into Jean-Marcel.

'Are you all right? You don't look so good.'

'Oh, just a few problems.'

'Come on, I told you mine, now you tell me yours,' said Jean-Marcel, leading him over to the bar.

In the lobby Hector noticed a half-finished glass of orange juice and remembered it was the only drink Vayla knew how to order.

They found themselves sitting at the bar, and as it was nearly evening they ordered a couple of Singapore Slings in memory of their visit to the temple.

'My friend has arrived from France,' explained Hector. 'She wants to see me.'

'Oh boy! And where's Vayla?'

'I don't know. I expect she's gone back to our room.'

'And what is it you want out of all this?'

This question amused Hector – it was the kind of thing he asked his patients. Had Jean-Marcel consulted one of his colleagues before?

'I don't know. I feel I love them both, but that's completely impossible. It's all the fault of the chemistry.'

'Chemistry?' Jean-Marcel asked, looking very intrigued.

'Yes, the chemistry of love, I mean. Little molecules spinning round in our heads like copulating mice . . . or ducks, for that matter.'

Jean-Marcel looked at Hector uneasily.

Just then a young man from reception came over and handed Hector an envelope. A letter a young woman had left for him, he explained.

Hector paused for a moment, but Jean-Marcel gestured to him to go ahead and open it. Hector took the letter out and began reading it, while Jean-Marcel sent a text message from his mobile.

I came, I saw and I was convinced. I ran into your beloved in the hotel lobby and I stayed a while to watch her. She is lovely – you have good taste – but then I already knew that. I can see how unbelievably lucky she must feel to have met you, which is good because you've always liked playing the role of saviour. I'm sorry, I'm being hurtful because I can't help feeling a bit jealous, even though I have no real right to after telling you I see no future for us. So I just hope you'll be happy, with her or with somebody else, but preferably with her because I'm already getting used to the idea. As for me, well, I might as well tell you before you hear it from someone else: I have another man in my life, too. I already know the horrible things you will think and I'm sure you'll come out with a few misogynistic remarks, but there it is. I'm having an affair with Gunther, but not for the reasons you might imagine.

My God, love is complicated. I feel miserable writing this, knowing you are with her, and at the same time I know I love Gunther. I send you my love, because I don't see why I wouldn't, but I don't think we should see each other for a while.

Clara

'Is everything all right?' asked Jean-Marcel.

Hector flushed with anger. Gunther. Gunther with his big two-faced grin. Gunther who had sent him on a mission to discover the secrets of love.

He leapt to his feet, coiled like a spring, ready to go to the ends of the earth to find Clara.

'Where are you going?'

'To the Peace Hotel.'

'Let's go there together!'

In the taxi, Jean-Marcel gave the driver the address, because, well, he spoke a bit of Chinese, too.

'Are you going to tell me what's making you so angry?' asked Jean-Marcel.

'My friend just told me she's leaving me for her boss.'

'Ah, I see . . .'

Outside, the Shanghai buildings glided past, like the ones in New York, as previously mentioned.

'I don't mean to be unkind,' said Jean-Marcel, 'but you aren't exactly behaving like a saint either.'

'It's only chemistry,' Hector repeated wearily.

And, at the same time, he felt it was unfair of him to reduce the gentle Vayla's love to a question of chemistry. Knowing how sensitive she was to his moods, how happy she was each time she saw him, and that they managed to joke with so few words. But how could he be sure?

Because he was very upset, and in psychiatry they teach you that talking helps, he explained to Jean-Marcel about the recent uncertainties in his relationship with Clara. Jean-Marcel listened very attentively, frowning.

'But why are we going to the Peace Hotel?'

'To find Clara.'

Jean-Marcel paused. 'Look, given the situation, I don't think that's a very good idea.'

'She's cheating on me with her boss!'

'Yes, all right. But let's just say she stopped loving you as much and now she loves someone else.'

'She's deceived me.'

'And what about you?'

'It's not the same. She had already told me things weren't working between us.'

'All right, but what will you gain from seeing her, especially in your present state?'

'She has come all the way to Shanghai. To see me!'

'Nevertheless, if I were you, I'd calm down first.'

Hector told himself that Jean-Marcel had taken on the role Hector usually had of helping people calm their emotions. But Hector was beginning to calm down. He had already considered the situation, and it was basically true that Clara had stopped loving him as much, and now she loved someone else. You can of course be angry with someone for that. (Some people are even driven to murder and Hector himself felt wound up enough to write something very blunt about the third component of heartache: anger!) But as love is involuntary, is it really fair to want to punish someone for a feeling over which they had no choice? In any case, Clara's letter had absolved him of the second component, guilt, he told himself as the taxi dropped them outside the Peace Hotel.

'You go ahead, I'll follow,' Jean-Marcel said, counting out the taxi fare.

Hector went through the revolving door, which so many celebrities had gone through so long ago. Two Chinese women dripping with jewellery came out as he went in. He thought:

Seedling no. 23: Love is like a revolving door; you go round and round, but you never manage to catch up with one another.

DO HECTOR AND CLARA STILL LOVE EACH OTHER?

CROUCHED like a huntress in the jungle behind a huge armchair upholstered with pouncing tigers, Vayla saw Hector enter the lobby of the Peace Hotel. He walked over to reception and asked something of one of the staff, who evidently didn't understand his pronunciation, unlike Vayla who understood everything. She had followed Clara to her hotel, out of a painful desire to dwell on her rival's superiority, and because she wanted to know more about this creature who posed such a threat to her.

She had seen Clara go up and was steeling herself for one of the most painful experiences of her life: seeing Hector join her in her room.

Just then, Clara appeared in the lobby, followed by a bellboy pulling her suitcase on a luggage trolley.

Clara and Hector noticed each other at the same moment. Hector took three steps forward, but Clara suddenly hid her face with one hand and, raising the other, gestured to him not to come near. Vayla instantly realised it wasn't a heartless gesture so much as the action of someone appealing for pity, as though speaking to Hector could only make her suffer even more. Hector stopped dead in his tracks while Clara, bowed down with grief, scarcely able to hold back her tears, walked towards the exit. Vayla went on deciphering the emotions on Hector's face as he stood motionless, and she certainly recognised pity, but also anger, and neediness. She was unaware that her own face was clouded by the same emotions.

Finally, Hector seemed to rouse himself and he caught up with Clara. He steered her over to a couch, not far from where Vayla was still hiding, unseen. Hector and Clara remained silent for a while. Clara dried her tears.

'How long has this been going on?' Hector asked.

Clara shrugged, as if the question were unimportant.

'A month, three months, six months?'

Clara made as if to get up and Hector realised he was taking the wrong approach.

'Well, all right, I'll have to live with that as well. With not knowing. At least tell me if you were already having an affair with him when we spent that weekend at your parents'?'

Clara bridled. 'No!'

Hector saw the tears still rolling down the face he loved so dearly. Love was truly terrible; how could two people who had once loved one another and who perhaps still loved one another inflict such suffering on each other?

'So why did you come to Shanghai?'

Clara shrugged, but this time as if laughing at herself.

'I have to go,' she said. 'My plane . . .'

'He could at least have let you fly in the company jet,' said Hector.

He felt pathetic for having said it – but too late.

He was torn between the urge to embrace Clara and the thought that you don't embrace a woman who has cheated on you.

And so he watched her cross the lobby and go outside, and his heart broke even more.

Jean-Marcel had seen the whole scene involving Clara, Hector and Vayla, and he slipped quietly out of a side exit, to go round and wait at the front of the hotel. He arrived just as Clara's taxi was leaving. He knew Vayla wouldn't come out from behind her armchair until Hector had left for his hotel. Jean-Marcel knew Asian women well. And that was one of his problems, because his wife suspected he knew them a bit too well.

In the taxi he said to Hector, 'You know, things aren't as bad as all that. I'm beginning to think you suffer from a rich man's worries.'

'Nonsense, she's in love with another man!'

'Hmm, she comes to Shanghai and cries as soon as she sees you.'

'That means she's attached to me, not that she still really loves me.'

'So being attached to someone isn't the same as being in love?'

Hector explained to Jean-Marcel the two main components of love according to Professor Cormorant.

(Hector thought there were others, but as they weren't clear to him yet he didn't mention them.) The first component: desire, passion, the urge to make love, indomitable dopamine. The first component could manifest itself from the first encounter (and disappear after the next for that matter). And then the second component, which often took a bit more time to develop, anywhere from a few hours to a few days: attachment, the desire to show affection towards the other, to have him or her near, a very strong but slightly calmer emotion, no doubt similar to the emotion between parents and children, the sweet taste of oxytocin. And one of the biggest problems with love was that these two components were often out of step, in one partner or the other or in both, and that is where Professor Cormorant and his drugs came in. (But he didn't talk to Jean-Marcel about that. Hector was on a mission, don't forget.) Explaining all this calmed Hector; it stopped him from thinking about Clara's tears.

'Well,' said Jean-Marcel, 'that's sort of what's happened to me and my wife. A lot of attachment, but not much desire. And during my trips, it's the exact reverse!'

'How is your interpreter, Madame Li?'

Jean-Marcel looked uncomfortable. 'Never mix business with pleasure,' he mumbled.

'Once you start saying that it's because they're already a bit mixed, isn't it?'

Jean-Marcel laughed slightly, and Hector knew he had fallen for his interpreter. When a man finds it difficult to talk about a woman, it is often a sign that he is in love with her. Because men – real men, traditional men, like Jean-Marcel – sense that love can weaken them. But ever since they were little they've been told they must always be strong.

Later, Hector felt sufficiently calm to begin writing, but he only had to say the name 'Gunther' from time to time and he would feel angry enough for it to cloud his inspiration.

HECTOR IS ANGRY

The Third Component of Heartache

The third component of heartache is anger. Unlike the second component, where we blame ourselves and all our faults for having driven the loved one away, this time it is the object of our love whom we blame for having behaved shamefully towards us. The person who has jilted us no longer seems to glow with boundless beauty and goodness, but appears on the contrary as a cruel, shallow, ungrateful being, in a word, a bitch, or a complete bastard, whom we would like to see, not as before in order to declare our undying love and our true remorse, but in order to unleash the full force of our wrath.

The third component manifests itself, then, in the form of painful fits of suppressed rage stirred by memories of all the loved one's failings, which take place most often in the final weeks before they leave. They break off contact for several days despite promising to stay in touch. With hindsight, there have been several indications that, before leaving us for good, they have been seeing someone else for an unknown period of time, the duration of which we will seek to discover with the doggedness of a palaeontologist attempting to date a dinosaur's jawbone. Shortly before withdrawing from us, they assure us tenderly that they love us. If they've lied to us, it shows how shamefully deceitful they are; if they meant what they had said, then they're shallow, fickle and irresponsible.

This resentment can become so intense it bursts out: we begin talking to ourselves, reproaching the loved one as though they were present, imagining them trembling, crying or begging for forgiveness when confronted with our righteous anger. One step further and we start leaving accusatory messages on the loved one's answering machine and voicemail, or writing them letters venting our anger in words aimed at hurting them in the same way as we have been hurt.

Hector paused. How could Clara have done this to him? Come to his bed at night and be having an affair with Gunther? He thought of several hurtful things he could have written straight away. But Hector stopped himself from emailing Clara. Hector is a psychiatrist, so perhaps he had learnt a little better than most that writing when you are in an emotional state never works very well. He went back to dealing with the third component.

These attempts at revenge are ill advised because after the email has been sent or the letter posted, we might suffer another unexpected attack of the second component (guilty brooding over our own past failings), which will be made all the more powerful by the sudden realisation that what we have just done is irreversible and renders impossible the return of the loved one, which, despite all signs to the contrary, is what we are still hoping for.

The act of writing had soothed Hector. He sensed there were still more components to deal with, but how many?

Suddenly he thought of old François. He seemed to have thought so much about heartache that Hector's reflections would surely interest him, and undoubtedly he would have his own ideas on the subject. Hector went on to the internet in order to send him his thoughts on the first three components.

He was still sitting at his computer when Vayla walked in and came to put her arm around his neck.

'*Noblem?*' she asked, ruffling his hair.

'*Noblem*,' replied Hector.

They looked at one another, and suddenly, for no reason, they burst out laughing. For a moment, Hector was surprised: he thought he had seen a tear in Vayla's eye.

HECTOR CALMS DOWN

LATER, they were sailing high up in the sky, but in a plane this time. Vayla complained of not being able to go to sleep on Hector's shoulder as the seats were too far apart, separated by huge armrests because, as you've guessed, Hector had not skimped on the price of the tickets – they were paid for by Gunther.

Since the armchair folded out into a proper bed, Vayla managed to drop off, settling, as she slept, into the position Hector loved so much. An *apsara* flies through the air, he thought.

He realised that Vayla, like most people from her country, had spent her childhood in one room where the whole family lived and where you slept next to each other, never alone. Where he came from, he knew psychiatrists talked a lot about the possible trauma children could suffer if they suddenly discovered their parents making love. But what if they had shared the same room since they were tiny? Were they permanently traumatised? And in that case were billions of the world's children permanently traumatised? And what if it was the other way round, what if people from countries like Hector's were traumatised by having been left all alone in a bedroom as babies, when, in the wild, animals of every species stay with their mothers? Of course, because countries like his had invented psychiatry, they were the ones who decided what was normal and what wasn't.

A few rows behind them (three to be precise, because in that part of the plane there aren't very many seats), he knew Jean-Marcel was talking to Not. Because, guess what, they were going back to Vayla and Not's country, where the professor was already waiting for them. And why not all travel in the same class: it was so much nicer, especially when you thought of Gunther's face when he had to explain the cost of the mission to his boss. (Because even Gunther has a boss, or people known as shareholders who can make trouble for him, so don't imagine the lives of big bosses are all plain sailing, because for a lot of them happiness is a question of comparison – they compare themselves with one another, their incomes, how big their companies are, a bit like little boys who enjoy seeing who can throw a stone the furthest or who has the biggest willy.)

Hector looked at the professor's message which Not had brought to him.

My dear friend,

We must flee – all has been exposed! I will tell you more in due course, but it appears Dr Wei brought some other associates on board, some new Chinese partners. I don't like collaborating with people who want to force me down new avenues of research, especially when they flash their gold teeth and watches at me, not to mention their bodyguards who come and flex their muscles in my little laboratory. As for the two youths, Wu and Lee, suddenly I'm not so sure what their game is; I even have my suspicions about their nationality and, I would venture to say, about their gender. No, don't think I've become paranoid . . . I already was, ha ha! In any event, this psychological tendency made me take steps that allowed me to erase the hard drive and deactivate the molecular samples in a jiffy, and, hey presto, Professor Cormorant vanishes into thin air, leaving in his wake only a big mouse orgy and a pair of lovesick ducks. Where have I gone? I shall leave it to the divine Not to inform the sublime Vayla. That's as safe a means of communication as the most secure networks: two apsaras *whispering in each other's ears; all you need to do is let yourself be guided!*

Best wishes,
Chester

P.S. I think Dr Wei's new partners are persistent (pig-headed) types. Take care nobody follows you.

These last words had prompted Hector to ask Jean-Marcel to go with them, and it was lucky because, as it happened, Jean-Marcel had to go back to Khmer country on business. (You may be wondering why we don't just say 'Cambodia' at this point. Well, it's because this is a story and in stories countries don't have names, unless they are fabulous thousand-year-old empires like China.)

Hector couldn't fall asleep because he kept thinking about Clara. He was experiencing the first three components – neediness, guilt and anger – consecutively or simultaneously. He calmed his neediness by looking at Vayla, assuaged his guilt by thinking of Gunther, stifled his anger by remembering Clara and his own past failings, and washed it all down with a few glasses of vintage champagne to take the edge off things. He could feel other components stirring in him, which made him a little uneasy, but at the same time he rejoiced at the prospect of penning a few sublime and probably immortal lines, which lovers would still be reading when all that remained of him was dust.

GUNTHER LOVES CLARA

It was Gunther's turn to feel needy and angry while he waited for Clara to return. (Didn't he feel any guilt? you may ask. Well, no, as a matter of fact he didn't. Gunther felt a sense of duty – towards his close family and friends – he was careful to avoid problems with his shareholders and the taxman, but guilt was not his strong point.)

What's more, Gunther was worried Clara might have told Hector about their relationship, and if that were the case, his incentive to find Professor Cormorant was likely to be severely diminished and Gunther's plans badly upset.

'What on earth is he doing?' wondered Gunther as he noticed the sudden appearance of large payments on the statements for the credit card they had given Hector, statements allowing them to track his movements, which were cross-checked and confirmed by other sources. The payments upset Gunther, not because of the actual sums of money, which were laughable compared to what he was used to handling, but because they weren't planned, and Gunther had always felt a strong need to control and to plan. Despite his passing irritation, Gunther never lost sight of the huge profits a drug enabling people to fall in love would generate.

Besides, constantly focusing on his aims was actually good for Gunther as it helped him not to suffer too much by thinking about Clara. Gunther sadly acknowledged that the one time he was truly in love with a woman, he was being punished for it. Up until then, he had experienced all his affairs and liaisons as a healthy distraction from the unhappiness of his home life. And yet Gunther loved his wife. Professor Cormorant would have said that what he felt was above all an attachment to the mother of his daughter, as well as a certain sense of duty: Gunther came from a traditional family where the men weren't always faithful but they never left their wives. How awful, some women will say, what a hypocrite, what amazing cowards men are. But if Gunther had left his wife and daughter to go and live with one of his pretty mistresses, would you find that praiseworthy and courageous? You see how complicated love is. Of course, we would prefer Gunther to remain faithful to his wife, but then the story wouldn't be so interesting anyway and, although big bosses who are completely faithful to their wives do exist, you'd have to look quite hard to find one.

On Hector's credit card statement Gunther noticed a very large payment to an Asian airline company renowned for its comfort. Is he travelling with his whole family or what? he thought. What annoyed Gunther even more was that, as part of a cost-control plan, the company executives were supposed to travel business class, not first class, and it was evident Hector was not only travelling first class himself, but was paying for others to travel first class.

His mobile rang. It was Clara.

'Are you calling from Shanghai?'

'From the airport.'

'Did you see him?'

'Yes.'

'Did you tell him about us?'

'Is this a cross-examination?'

Like Hector, Gunther sensed he was taking the wrong approach. It's a tendency men have, always to ask very precise questions about facts, whereas women feel that truth lies beyond mere facts.

'I'm sorry,' he said, 'I get very anxious when you're away from me. I miss you terribly.'

'I miss you, too,' said Clara.

They carried on saying affectionate things to each other, and at the same time Gunther could sense Clara was upset; she wasn't talking to him the way she normally did. She's told him everything, he thought. She's told him everything.

As he was talking to Clara, Gunther looked at his diary, ticking off all the meetings he could cancel so that he could fly to Asia immediately. This was an emergency.

'Stay there,' he said. 'I'm on my way.'

HECTOR AND THE LITTLE MOUNTAIN FAIRIES

A MUFFLED sound came from the forest.

'Is that a monkey?' asked Hector.

'No, it's a tiger,' said Jean-Marcel. 'On the prowl.'

They decided it was best to go back to the car, a big four-wheel drive they had hired for an exorbitant sum. Vayla and Not had stayed in the back seat; they knew they were in tiger territory because this was their country!

'Your friend the professor doesn't believe in making things easy, does he?' said Jean-Marcel. 'Burying himself in a little village in the mountains. I'm not even sure we'll be able to do the last few miles in the car.'

'What about the tigers?' Hector asked.

'Oh, there'll be fewer at this altitude.'

Fewer. This reminded Hector of the time he had wanted to go for a swim in a tropical sea. He had asked a friend who lived there whether there were sharks. The friend had replied, 'Hardly ever.' Hector had gone for a swim, but it was a very short one.

Anyway, he had noticed that the ever-practical Jean-Marcel had a gun holster in his luggage, as well as a box containing a satellite phone and receiver, which would enable him to keep up with his business affairs and to access the internet. Hector thought he might be able to send a message to Clara when they arrived, although he wondered what he could possibly write to her.

The road wasn't very good, and it wasn't even really a road any more, more of a track, and not even a proper track in places. The forest began to thin out – it wasn't jungle any more, but more like a forest in Hector's country, only with trees that were sometimes different.

In the back, Vayla and Not were speaking in excited voices. This was the first time in their lives they had been sightseeing in their own country and they seemed to be enjoying it enormously.

'You look more relaxed,' said Jean-Marcel.

'Hmm,' said Hector, 'I tell myself some problems have no solution, so what's the point of even trying to find one?'

'You're beginning to think like a local. If you're not careful, you'll end up staying here.'

Hector looked at the hills covered with trees, some of the green slopes partially hidden by patches of early-morning mist. And why not stay here? Set up home in one of the long wooden houses on stilts he had seen from the road, with Vayla.

But he knew even Vayla wouldn't have been keen on the idea. Like all women, or nearly all women, she preferred living in a town than in the middle of the countryside.

'My God,' said Jean-Marcel, 'we should have been there ages ago by now.'

They were driving along the side of a huge bare hill – you might even have said a small mountain – and on the other side you could see a forest, but apart from that there was nothing, only a few tiny paddy fields dotted here and there where the land was a little flatter, like ornaments on an already magnificent landscape.

Jean-Marcel turned round to show Not and Vayla the map and ask them where they were, but judging from the panic on their faces, it was obvious they didn't know how to read a map, and in this they were no different from Clara, thought Hector. Still, Jean-Marcel could understand a bit of Khmer.

'Not and Vayla say the problem with these villages is they sometimes move around.'

'Why?'

'These people practise slash-and-burn farming. So some years they have to move to a different area. Otherwise their paddy fields become barren. Or it brings bad luck and they have to please the gods. Or the tigers—'

'But if there are paddy fields, the villages can't be far away.'

Jean-Marcel shrugged as if to say, you never know here, and it was sort of true, because they didn't even know what country they were in. This area was on the border between three different countries which had once been colonised by Hector's country, and when his fellow countrymen had left (with a bit of persuasion, it has to be said), they took with them the layouts showing the exact position of the frontiers in the mountains, and as there weren't any real landmarks – no high peaks or wide rivers, just a few villages that moved around – the three countries weren't too sure where their borders were, and for that matter they didn't try too hard to find out.

An hour earlier, they had bumped into a small patrol of soldiers from one of the countries, who had asked to see their papers, and Hector had noticed that Jean-Marcel's passport looked thicker than usual when he handed it to them, and thin again when they handed it back, and they had driven off without a problem, watching the soldiers in the rear-view mirror jumping for joy. Jean-Marcel had said this technique worked very well with soldiers from one of the three countries, and not at all with those from one of the other two, but for that country he had brought along some official documents. That was the good thing about his business – he knew quite a lot of people.

All these little incidents distracted Hector and kept him from thinking about the fourth and fifth components of heartache, which occurred to him every time he imagined spending the rest of his life without Clara. It kept happening, but he managed to dispel the thoughts by glancing at Vayla, who had fallen asleep leaning against Not, who was also asleep. He had never met a woman who had such a calming effect on him when he looked at her, no doubt an effect of Professor Cormorant's modified oxytocin molecule. Maybe taking another dose would cure him of Clara. But that would mean making a commitment to Vayla. Commitment, there was a word Professor Cormorant never talked about in relation to love.

They saw three figures walking along the track and, what a surprise, it was three little girls, almost young ladies, who stopped to watch them as they approached.

They were dressed in tunics embroidered with delicately coloured flowers, and bright-red little headdresses that were magnificent above their charming faces. They were walking barefoot in the dust, but looked as elegant as if they were in a fashion parade. They had an impressive calm about them, and yet you could see how astonished they were at the arrival of this carload of strangers. The sight of the young girls sent Not and Vayla into paroxysms of delight. Jean-Marcel stopped the car to allow them to ask their young fellow countrywomen the way. In fact, they weren't exactly fellow countrywomen because it was clear they didn't speak the same language. Hector had read in a guidebook the day before that the Gna-Doas, the tribe to which these three little mountain fairies obviously belonged, spoke a language only they knew, which came from Upper Tibet, the country they had left long ago, driven out by the cold and by other less friendly tribes.

In the end, Vayla and Not invited the three little mountain fairies to climb into the back of the car with them and, once they had sat down, they bubbled over with girlish joy, laughing and chattering like delightful multicoloured birds.

Another moment of happiness, thought Hector.

Then the eldest began directing Jean-Marcel, giving him little taps on the shoulder. She wasn't very old, but she already had a sense of authority.

'If my wife really does leave me,' said Jean-Marcel, 'I'll settle down here, start a transport business, set up a health clinic and marry a local girl. No more problems.'

Hector understood. Being there in the middle of those mountains made them feel very removed from their own world, a bit like when you go to the countryside but multiplied by a thousand. But Hector knew this sort of emotion can be deceptive, and you end up missing what you are used to, and building a lasting relationship with a local girl would be different but no easier than with a woman from his own country, because it was still about people and that mysterious alchemy of love. Unless of course you had some of Professor Cormorant's drugs, which was a very tempting solution.

At a bend in the track, houses on stilts appeared on a hillside, in the middle of a clearing. Hector glimpsed young people pounding rice in large bowls, and old men sitting on the doorsteps of their houses smoking pipes. A few pigs and chickens wandered about. At the sound of the car engine, everybody looked up to watch them arrive.

'Kormoh!' cried Not.

Professor Cormorant, dressed in a long flowery tunic, rushed over, smiling, to greet them.

HECTOR WRITES IN THE DARK

LATE in the evening, stretched out on a mat in a Gna-Doa house on stilts, Hector was writing in the dark, with the computer screen as his only light. Vayla was asleep, her body pressed against his, out of love and a desire for warmth. Outside was silence, the immense silence of the mountain regions.

The Fourth Component of Heartache

The fourth component of heartache is loss of self-esteem. The departure of the loved one is a huge blow to your self-esteem, because does it not show that once people get to know you, you lose your attractiveness? After a few weeks or months or years with you it was inevitable that the loved one, an exceptional being, would end up discovering and being revolted by your mediocrity, which you only managed to disguise long enough to seduce them, and which only their inexperience prevented them from detecting. Now that you find yourself without them, all your old inadequacies – physical, moral, intellectual and social – which you were able to forget or to put into perspective, now seem like insurmountable weaknesses.

Hector stopped writing. He couldn't help thinking of Gunther, and the differences between him and a big businessman like Gunther appeared to him as so many personal failings. He had observed the same response in everyone who was jilted, with a slight variation: women were often obsessed by their rival's physique (even when there was nothing better about her) and men by the social status or the showiness of the one who had stolen their beloved (even when there was nothing better about him). His training as a psychiatrist reminded him that he could, however, look at the flip side: he, too, had attracted women who were no longer in love with their Gunthers and he, too, might have seemed like an exciting Gunther who had come along and disrupted a boring relationship. But the intensity of what he was experiencing in the moment prevailed over reason. And he couldn't boost his self-esteem by thinking of Vayla, because he knew their love, although genuine, had been sparked off by a modified molecule. He went on writing.

> *Evidently, such shortcomings condemn you to a life of perpetual solitude, or to accepting second best and mourning the loved one forever. (At this point in your reflections, beware of being assailed by the first and second components.) The love you experienced with the loved one was a stroke of luck that you didn't deserve and that you were unable to make last anyway, a paradise you were only granted access to because the loved one was overly generous towards you. You enjoyed a smug sense of superiority so long as you didn't leave your mediocre world, like a big*

fish in a small pond, but your pursuit of the loved one led you out into the open sea of sentiment, where only the very best can hope to survive. The unbearable pain you feel now is only just atonement for your inadequacy combined with your vanity.

Well, now he was exaggerating a bit – he didn't feel quite that inadequate. He began to fall asleep, comforted by the soothing sound of Vayla's breathing.

Hector was suddenly all ears. The house they had been allotted was at the edge of the village. Would the stilts stop a tiger from getting in?

He felt the bamboo floor shake beneath him, he heard a commotion in the darkness and was about to throw his computer at it (would the tiger be scared off by this attack with an unknown weapon?) when someone lit a paraffin lamp and Jean-Marcel appeared, looking half asleep, his hair dishevelled.

'Did you hear that?'

'Yes.'

They listened and heard the murmur of human voices coming from the neighbouring houses.

'Apparently, during the hunting season tigers don't come into the villages,' Jean-Marcel said. 'Or if they do they only attack the buffaloes.'

Further away, they could hear the buffaloes lowing softly in their dark stable.

Jean-Marcel crouched in the doorway, which was open to the night, and Hector saw he was carrying a Gna-Doa rifle, an old gun made at the village forge. He had a contented air about him.

Hector opened his computer again. He wrote:

Seedling no. 24: Nothing eases the pain of love better than focusing on a task.

HECTOR MEETS HIS COUSINS

Ouuuu-ouuuu.

It was a plaintive, almost human cry that emanated from the forest in front of them, and thrilled Professor Cormorant.

'They're there! They're there!' he whispered excitedly.

They were walking in single file along a little pathway that disappeared into the undergrowth in places. Leading the way was Aang-long-arms, a strapping lad from the village who, it seemed, was always happy to go off on an expedition, followed by Professor Cormorant, Hector and Jean-Marcel, who still had his rifle from the night before.

They had left just after dawn, which, apparently, reduced the risk of a tiger attack, and anyway tigers *rarely* attack a group of adults. A fine mist still clung to the mountainsides, pierced occasionally by golden rays of morning sunlight.

Finally, Aang gestured to them not to make a noise, and they moved forward very slowly, half crouching.

Through a screen of trees, Hector glimpsed a mass of orange fur, then clearly made out an enormous ape, idly scratching its armpits. He recognised the hairless face, the thoughtful, calm expression, the muscular torso and arms, and the little bent legs of an orang-utan.

'That's the female,' breathed Professor Cormorant. 'I call her Mélisande.'

Just then, another orang-utan dropped out of the trees, landing deftly beside Mélisande, who paid no attention to him as he looked around uneasily. He was slightly bigger and perhaps a bit more muscular than her.

'That's Pelléas, the male.'

Pelléas moved closer to Mélisande and began sniffing her muzzle, but she turned away and went on scratching herself with sullen indifference. Pelléas changed tactics and began scratching her back. Mélisande's face lit up instantly and she turned her head towards Pelléas, over her shoulder, and they gave each other a little – er – kiss.

'You'll notice Pelléas is only marginally bigger than Mélisande,' whispered the professor, 'as in all monogamous species. The bigger the male in proportion to the female the more polygamous the species!'

Aang gestured to him to be quiet, but slightly too late. Pelléas and Mélisande had broken off their tender exchanges and were looking towards them with angry little eyes.

'*Aou-ou?*' Pelléas bellowed.

Without further ado, Mélisande shot off into the trees, Pelléas stood up roaring and beat his chest with his enormous fists, then, all of a sudden, in two bounds and three movements of his arms, he vanished into the foliage after Mélisande.

'We scared them away,' said Jean-Marcel.

Aang-long-arms made a gesture signalling a rapid retreat, then said, laughing, '*Khrar!*' It was the only Gna-

Doa word that had immediately stuck in Hector's mind and it meant 'tiger'.

'Tigers hunt them, so they're on their guard.'

'There you see the future!' Professor Cormorant resumed. 'An animal closely related to us – you know the old cliché, ninety-eight per cent of genes in common with humans – and at the same time completely monogamous. Orang-utans mate for life! Good God, they are the only Catholic ape!' he declared, bursting out laughing.

Aang-long-arms laughed too, everybody found Professor Cormorant very funny, even people who couldn't speak his language.

'You see,' said Professor Cormorant, 'the little pills, fiddling with hormones, that's all child's play. The real future is in gene therapy. Discovering the genes that determine the structures in the orang-utan's brain – I mean the ones responsible for this lasting attachment, not the ones that make him go *ou-ou*!'

'And what if you find those genes?'

'Well, I shall incorporate them into our genetic heritage and we will become a monogamous, faithful species, as will our children. What do you say to that, eh?'

'It's very interesting,' said Jean-Marcel. 'And are there people working on it?'

'In any case, it's a good place to start,' said Professor Cormorant.

'I thought Sumatra had the most orang-utans,' said Hector.

'Yes, but they also have government agencies, inspectors, the State – in short, problems. Here, it's a sort of no-man's land, or rather a place where there are only intelligent, hospitable people like good old Aang and his fellow countrymen. I am going to send for equipment and—'

Suddenly, Aang motioned with his hand and began very carefully scanning the forest. Everybody was quiet.

Aang and Jean-Marcel raised their rifles.

A few yards away, the undergrowth was moving slightly. A large creature appeared to be coming towards them through the vegetation. Then the movements of the branches separated; there must be two smaller animals, one following the other. Then they heard a faint cry of pain, unmistakably human this time.

'Who goes there?' demanded Jean-Marcel.

Aang repeated the same thing in his language.

The branches stopped moving, there was another rustle of foliage and Miko and Chizourou appeared dressed in rain hats and camouflage gear, looking very embarrassed.

HECTOR IS AN ETHNOLOGIST

'It doesn't look very alcoholic,' said Hector.

'Appearances can be deceptive,' said Jean-Marcel.

Hector thanked the village chief, Gnar, a wizened little man who had just plunged a bowl into an earthenware jar of fermented rice wine and was handing it to him with a smile.

'*À vot'santé*,' he said, because he knew a few expressions in Hector's language, passed down to him by his grandfather, who had apparently been somewhat on the side of Hector's fellow countrymen back in the days when they occupied the countries in that region. In honour of the occasion, Gnar had put on an old white cap, which gave him a very majestic air.

Besides this, he had an intelligent look in his eyes, a wife his own age and another younger than him – his deceased brother's wife, so Hector had gathered – and a very loud voice when he got annoyed with the young people for doing stupid things. He and the professor seemed very friendly and kept clinking bowls. The professor whispered to Hector that he had given Chief Gnar some of his compound A drugs.

Everyone was sitting on the bamboo floor of a large communal house on stilts, around some earthenware jars people had brought. The women, all wearing embroidered tunics, sat at a slight distance talking amongst themselves, like a big bouquet of flowery fabric. They drank noticeably less than the men and seemed very intrigued by Vayla and Not, who had been given traditional costumes to wear. As evening was setting in, the children were also inside, playing at the far end of the long room.

Gnar had gathered Hector, Jean-Marcel and Professor Cormorant, the honoured guests, around him, and even Miko and Chizourou, who in turn also had to drink fermented rice wine. Outside, you could see the sun setting over the mountains in a symphony of delicate golden tints and hazy blues.

Miko and Chizourou looked a little uneasy amidst all those men; even so they smiled as they said '*Haong-zao-tu*', which for the Gna-Doas meant Happy New Year, let the harvest be plentiful, let the tigers stay away and let there be no war.

Aang-long-arms suddenly stood up and began singing a song, which was received with cries of joy, including from the children.

Professor Cormorant leaned over to Hector. 'Isn't life here wonderful?'

'How do they cope with love?'

'They have very complex laws. I can't remember exactly, hang on.'

He leaned over to Chief Gnar and asked him a question. Gnar smiled and gave quite a lengthy reply.

'That's right, here everyone calls everyone else brother and sister if they share a maternal ancestor, and as a rule they aren't allowed to intermarry, unless some of their biological uncles have already married their fathers' nieces or, at a stretch, their cousins' mother-in-laws' children. You see, it's not simple.'

'No. They need a good memory.'

'But, other than that, they can make love with anyone they like, provided they don't get caught!'

And he burst out laughing.

'And if they do get caught?'

'In those cases, the guilty party is forced to borrow money to buy a buffalo, which is sacrificed to prevent the village from being cursed. But the gods will only curse the village if you get caught – that's what I like about Gna-Doa law!'

'Do couples stay together?'

'Yes.'

'What's their secret?'

'Unlike other tribes, they no longer have forced marriages, a source of much unhappiness. Here the man makes his request through the chief, who acts as an intermediary with the girl's family. The family may accept the man's request or not, but the girl has the right to refuse. And then they have a very interesting custom: between the acceptance of the request and the marriage ceremony, the betrothed couple are allowed to spend a night together, after which the girl may still refuse. The Gna-Doas understand the importance of physical love, especially during the early stages of a relationship . . .'

'What about later on? How do they make love last?'

This question seemed absolutely crucial to Hector. Almost everyone could fall in love at some point in their lives, but by no means everyone was able to make love last.

Professor Cormorant gestured to the children and young people a small distance away towards the back of the room.

'Here, they live together all the time, they bring up their children together, everybody does his or her share of the work, couples spend very little time alone, unlike where we come from. They would find the idea of a man and a woman alone in their little apartment every evening completely crazy! Maybe the way to make love last is by not spending too much time alone together.'

'At the same time, we would find that lack of privacy intolerable,' said Hector.

'Because we've been brought up like that, each in our own room, but look at them,' Professor Cormorant said, pointing at the children, who did seem rather happy, it has to be said.

Just then, the young girls they had met on the road stood up and walked over to three boys their own age. One boy was holding a sort of flute and one of the girls a long two-stringed guitar.

The circle widened to give them room.

There was silence as they began to play, the flute's soft lament seeming to wrap itself around the guitar's thin notes, while their friends danced gracefully on the spot, smiling and spinning on their tiny feet.

Hector felt very moved at the sight of this calm happiness, which suddenly seemed to him so easy to attain. He and Vayla exchanged glances; she smiled at him, and he said to himself that, with or without chemistry, they loved each other.

The children stopped and everyone cheered. They bowed modestly and did a few more dance steps before rejoining their group.

'Isn't it magnificent?' whispered Professor Cormorant. 'I know of ethnologists who would give an arm and a leg to see this!'

Hector agreed, but he was beginning to be more interested in Japanese ethnology. As a result of drinking the bowls of fermented rice wine the chief had given them, Miko and Chizourou's cheeks had turned bright pink, like two little geishas on a spree. To explain what they were doing in Gna-Doa country they had said that the big environmental organisation they worked for had sent them there to check up a bit on the conditions of orang-utans in that region. None of this was entirely convincing as, in that type of organisation, it is seldom the same people taking care of ruined temples and endangered species – but because in Asia you must always be very polite and allow people to save face, Hector, Jean-Marcel and Professor Cormorant pretended to believe them, and Miko and Chizourou pretended to believe they believed them, and they pretended to believe they believed they believed them, and so on, but they still seemed quite uneasy.

Through a haze of alcohol, Hector glimpsed a small purple stone sparkling in Miko's ear. And suddenly he remembered: it was identical to the one he had seen young Lu wearing in Shanghai. The East certainly is mysterious, he thought, because he was becoming too tired to have any original thoughts, but deep down he had understood, which shows that fermented rice wine didn't affect his inner mind.

But later, Chief Gnar went away and came back with two bottles that looked as if they came from another era. On the faded labels, the edges of which had been nibbled away by several generations of insects, you could make out a young native woman smiling beneath a cone-shaped hat and, above, the words: *Siam and Tonkin General Distillery Company*.

'*Choum-choum!*' said Gnar with a big smile.

'Ah, this is going to do some damage!' said Jean-Marcel.

HECTOR AND THE RISING SUN

HECTOR awoke at dawn. Jean-Marcel's loud snores reverberated from the other side of the room.

Vayla was still sleeping, on her side, as though she were trying out a different pose for the sculptor who in her dream was immortalising her on a temple wall.

The air was chilly. Hector slid the ladder down, taking care not to make a noise, and descended cautiously because Gna-Doa ladders only have one central pole, and woe betide the clumsy.

He noticed some women already at work in the paddy fields where a few patches of mist lingered, while others sat weaving in the doorways of their house. A few small children were busy gathering up rice husks. The men hadn't appeared yet. Professor Cormorant had explained that the Gna-Doas only drank alcohol on traditional feast days, but Hector had understood that there were quite a few of these in their calendar.

He walked over to the house where he knew Miko and Chizourou were staying. Their ladder was down, and he climbed up without making a sound. He heard a whispered conversation in Japanese, or thought he did anyway.

Standing next to their big backpacks, the two young Japanese women were clearly preparing to leave. They jumped when they saw Hector, and were even more surprised when he greeted them by the names Lu and Wee. Then they looked at each other. And Hector understood that Chizourou, the one who supposedly spoke no English at the temple, was probably Miko's boss.

Hector thought he must put them at their ease and he said he would tell them some interesting things provided they explained to him who they really were. And, moreover, as he already had his suspicions, they only stood to gain from this exchange.

He found himself sitting cross-legged like them – which was very uncomfortable for him, but he didn't want to appear in a position of inferiority – listening to Chizourou, who, it turned out, spoke perfect English. She'd studied at Emmanuel College, Cambridge. She explained that they really did work for a big non-governmental organisation concerned with nature conservation. And this organisation was interested in Professor Cormorant's research, because his results might help endangered species to breed in captivity, like the pandas at Shanghai Zoo. And, incidentally, that cuddly animal was their organisation's logo!

Hector said this was all very interesting, but if they were telling him tall stories he could tell them even taller ones. What's more, he wondered whether the endangered species that most interested Miko and Chizourou wasn't in fact Japanese babies. And he added that when people didn't tell him the truth he felt under no obligation to tell them the truth.

There was another little whispered exchange between Miko and Chizourou, and this time Miko admitted that, all right, there was some truth in this story about the Japanese babies. The Japanese population was getting dangerously old and one of the reasons for this was that young women were having fewer and fewer babies, and this was more and more because they were remaining single, she explained.

'Japanese men too macho,' said Chizourou, who also spoke a bit of Hector's language, but not very well. 'Women modern! Japanese men work too much, go out always with other men, drink saké, karaoke, come home drunk, behave not nice! Japanese women prefer stay single, go on holiday with women friends! Good job, earn money, no need for men!'

And Hector remembered that in his country it was true that most Japanese tourists were in fact young females travelling in pairs, like Miko and Chizourou.

And so the Japanese government was very interested in a drug that would make men and women stay in love with each other, which would produce new generations of Japanese babies brought up in a happy loving environment.

Hector remembered the speech made by Dr Wei, the important Chinese man in Shanghai. Professor Cormorant's drug, far from being a potion intended for personal happiness, could have important consequences for the fate of a nation, perhaps even for humanity itself.

But Miko interrupted these reflections. Now it was Hector's turn, what could he tell them?

Hector had begun explaining laboriously in English about oxytocin and dopamine when Vayla's worried face appeared in the doorway, followed by her graceful body as she reached the top of the ladder and walked over to them with quick, determined steps. Hector drew her to him and she slipped into a sitting position between his legs, leaning back against him as if she were in an armchair.

'As I was saying,' Hector resumed.

Miko and Chizourou looked very impressed.

They glanced at one another again and then Chizourou asked whether they might not be able to take one of Professor Cormorant's drugs, on a trial basis. Hector was about to say they would have to take it with their respective fiancés, but suddenly he realised Miko and Chizourou might not be just fellow workers any more.

There really were a lot of people interested in Professor Cormorant's research.

HECTOR BLOWS SOMEONE'S COVER

JEAN-MARCEL was lighting a fire outside, watched by a group of Gna-Doa children who followed his every movement with interest.

'Aren't they adorable?' he said to Hector.

And with their bright smiling faces and flower-patterned clothes that were like something out of an oriental fairy tale, the children looked like perfect miracles who should be protected forever from television advertising and factory-made sweets.

'You seem in a good mood,' said Hector.

'Yes, I hooked up the satellite dish and I've been able to exchange a few emails with my wife.'

'And what does she say?'

'Some rather nice things. She says she's reinventing herself. Do you understand what that means?'

'That she's building herself anew, like building a new house to welcome you home again.'

'Excellent! I really hope you're right.'

'What about your Chinese interpreter?'

'Well, in the end nothing happened.'

Jean-Marcel explained that he and Madame Li had felt very attracted to one another, and had even confided their feelings over two glasses of iced green tea, but finally they had decided it was wiser not to endanger the relationships they were each trying to patch up.

'That's wonderful!' said Hector.

'Possibly,' said Jean-Marcel. 'But it's not easy. Though I have the feeling I've grown up a bit. It's the first time in my life I've voluntarily turned down a promising and very tempting affair.'

Hector thought this type of self-denial was probably one of the noblest demonstrations of love, even though it usually had to remain a secret. You can't go home and say: 'Darling, I nearly had a passionate affair, but I love you so much I stopped myself at the last minute.' Because, for many people, ideal love would be not being tempted, even for a second, but does that kind of love really exist? In the end, isn't resisting temptation more meaningful than not being tempted at all?

He opened his little notebook and wrote: *Loving someone means resisting temptation.*

Vayla had come up to them and was watching him with interest as he wrote. Hector sensed that she longed to understand the meaning of his notes, as if then she could be sure of always understanding him.

'I ought to tell you Vayla asked to use my computer to send an email in Khmer to someone at the hotel. I think the letter is meant for you, and she is waiting for an English translation to be sent back.'

Vayla had understood what they were talking about, and she smiled at Hector with the gleeful look of someone who has just played a good trick on you.

‘Where are the Japanese girls?’ Jean-Marcel asked.

‘They were leaving, but decided to stay on a bit longer.’

‘They’re funny tourists,’ Jean-Marcel said.

‘And you’re a funny businessman,’ Hector said.

Jean-Marcel didn’t respond and went on busying himself with the fire.

‘Do you want me to tell you what they told me?’ asked Hector. ‘So you can put it in your report to Gunther.’

Jean-Marcel froze. He didn’t reply. Then he smiled. ‘Well, there’s no need to pretend any more, is there?’

‘No, there’s no need.’

‘Only I’d rather Gunther didn’t find out you’ve blown my cover. Can I ask you not to mention it to him for the time being?’

‘Agreed.’

Jean-Marcel seemed relieved, and that surprised Hector. He said to himself that a real professional would never allow his cover, as he called it, to be blown so easily. Confronted by Hector, who only had unfounded suspicions, Jean-Marcel could have denied everything and possibly persuaded Hector he was being paranoid. Hector thought that Jean-Marcel had probably allowed one false cover to be blown in order to hide another. He couldn’t be working for Gunther. Hector thought of Captain Lin Zaou of the People’s Liberation Army, and Dr Wei, and then of Miko and Chizourou’s real employers. Wasn’t this affair becoming a bit too serious for a psychiatrist suffering the torments of love?

Just then, Not arrived looking very worried.

'*Kormoh*? *Kormoh*?'

And behind her came Chief Gnar and Aang-long-arms, looking equally worried. Professor Cormorant had disappeared.

THE PROFESSOR AND THE ORANG-UTAN

'YOU know,' whispered Jean-Marcel, 'they were mainly relying on me to look out for you, not really to inform on you. After all, you're the one who's supposed to be sending reports.'

They were walking together in the forest, in the middle of a row of beaters – all men from the tribe. Everyone was worried Professor Cormorant might have got lost going to study the orang-utans.

'I hope he didn't run into a tiger,' said Jean-Marcel.

'I think he would throw even a tiger off balance.'

It was odd but the discovery of Jean-Marcel's true role hadn't diminished Hector's fondness for him. Perhaps the fact that they had shared powerful emotions – the mine in the temple, their problems with their respective partners – had forged a sort of bond between them. He was also curious about Jean-Marcel's real mission. Was it to kidnap the professor and take him for questioning at the secret offices of an even more secret service? Was it to get hold of the samples and the contents of the hard disks?

This whole mission of spying on the professor seemed of secondary importance to Hector. His main concern was to get hold of a dose of antidote. But to what end, ultimately? In order to take the antidote with Vayla?

Why not take it with Clara instead? Mightn't the antidote help them separate? That was one application Professor Cormorant hadn't thought of: using chemistry to break a natural but painful bond. An end to heartache, and all the literature it gave rise to.

In front of him, Jean-Marcel motioned to him to stop.

Twenty yards ahead of them, in a small clearing, Professor Cormorant was crouching, whispering to two orang-utans, who were watching him with interest.

'He's crazy,' said Jean-Marcel. 'He has no idea.'

Hector had noticed the professor was holding two balls of rice paste, probably containing new drugs, and was gradually edging closer to the two enormous primates. Pelléas (for it was he) suddenly seemed unhappy about this growing proximity and let out a low roar. The professor, completely unfazed, slowly stretched out his hand, offering him the rice ball. Pelléas kept growling insistently, letting it be known that he was ready to step up the level of aggression.

At that moment, Hector realised that, beside him, Jean-Marcel was taking aim at the animal, not with a Gna-Doa musket but with a very modern-looking rifle.

It was Mélisande who suddenly leapt towards the professor, snatched the rice ball and immediately swallowed it. Pelléas instantly hurled himself at the professor, knocking him down as he snatched the other rice ball. In a flash, the two animals vanished into the trees.

Jean-Marcel's forehead was bathed in sweat. 'My God! I was this close to . . .'

Professor Cormorant lay flat on the ground, motionless. They rushed over to him. He was having difficulty breathing.

'My friends . . .' he whispered.

Hector leaned over to examine him and diagnosed a broken rib or two resulting from his brief collision with Pelléas. Pelléas had probably only wanted to scare this strange white-haired cousin in his orang-utan way, which had caught the professor off guard, for, whilst admittedly young in spirit, he was actually rather elderly and weighed less than nine stone.

GUNTHER IS SCARED

'WHY did you come?' asked Clara.

'This mission is slipping out of control. I wanted to keep an eye on things.'

'Keep an eye on what things? On me? On him?'

'On the mission.'

'Are you going to see him?'

'Yes, I'm going to see him.'

'I told him about us, you know.'

'That hardly makes things easier, does it?'

'Would you have preferred me never to tell him? Would you have preferred him not to know? Did you just want to keep me as a secret little pleasure for after work?'

'No, of course not, but it wasn't the right time.'

'Oh, really? But it was the right time for us to start an affair?'

'Listen . . .'

'Our shenanigans have not really been the best thing for our work, have they? We should have waited a few years, until I moved to another company, right? Then we could have said to ourselves, okay, now's the right time! We could have synchronised our schedules.'

'You're being ridiculous. You always have to exaggerate.'

Gunther and Clara were lying on two steamer chairs made of tropical wood beside a swimming pool in the middle of a heavenly garden with a magnificent view over the forest and the mountains in the distance. To the left, the golden pinnacles of a temple emerged through the leaves . . . It looked like paradise, but it felt a bit like hell, or at least that was what Gunther was thinking.

They were waiting for some suitable means of transport to be arranged that would get them quickly to where Hector and the professor were. Gunther's two associates who had accompanied him on this trip were somewhere in the hotel frantically arranging this with the company's local representative.

Gunther looked at Clara stretched out beside him, her face hidden behind an enormous pair of sunglasses that gave her an inscrutable air, her adorable body tanning in the sun. She was clearly still angry but that did not prevent him from realising that the true reason for his sudden trip to Asia was to be able to spend some time alone with her, or almost alone with her.

He was desperately in love. What was happening to him for heaven's sake! Was this an effect of ageing? He was twelve years older than Hector, and had noticed that some very young women didn't look at him the way they used to; he sensed they no longer imagined him as a potential lover – it didn't even cross their minds – and as a result they were far more friendly and relaxed in his company. He wasn't as strong as he used to be – he could feel it – and if that little wild cat lying there next to him sensed it she would start ripping him to shreds.

Gunther the Downsizer was in danger of being downsized.

Unless . . .

Professor Cormorant's potion. What if he made the little wild cat take it? She would refuse of course, but she didn't have to know. According to the latest report, the attachment drug came in liquid form, easy to slip into someone's glass without them realising.

Gunther felt his hopes soar. This research, which had cost so much money and caused so many problems, might be about to have its first positive result: binding Clara to him forever.

At the same time, he sensed such an action would torment him. Gunther's strict upbringing had taught him always to win fairly. The thought that he might be capable of cheating gave rise to an unfamiliar feeling in him: guilt. But, after all, he could easily find a psychiatrist to help him get over that.

HECTOR IS A GOOD DOCTOR

'PELLÉAS didn't mean it, ouch!'

'Don't talk too much,' said Hector. 'Just concentrate on breathing.'

It was a piece of advice Professor Cormorant found difficult to follow, even though the pain was a sharp reminder every time he tried to talk. He was lying on a mat in the dark in Chief Gnar's house. The chief was gazing at him apologetically because a chief feels responsible for the well-being of his guests, however foolhardy they may be. Other men from the tribe were standing around the injured man, solemnly discussing what had happened. At any rate, that is what you would assume if you weren't familiar with the languages of Upper Tibet.

Not had slipped a tapestry cushion under the professor's head and was lovingly holding his hand. Vayla was sitting next to him fanning the air above his face with a big leaf. Except for the professor's ashen complexion, they made a charming picture for anyone nostalgic for the Orient.

Hector and Jean-Marcel moved away a little so they could talk.

'He looks dreadful.'

'The pain is making it hard for him to breathe.'

Hector was concerned. Professor Cormorant had just told him he only had one and a half lungs, the result of a Jeep accident in his youth, when he was doing his military service. He had broken the ribs on the side of his good lung, which fortunately hadn't been punctured. Hector had checked this by examining him thoroughly, but the professor's already diminished lung capacity had been even further reduced.

Jean-Marcel, normally so well prepared, had only a few ordinary painkillers in his first-aid kit, and these didn't seem to do much to ease the professor's discomfort, even though his chest had been tightly bandaged, on Hector's instructions. The pain would probably remain severe for the next forty-eight hours. Taking the professor by car to the nearest town seemed impossible, because the bumpy road would be agonising for him. Evacuating him by helicopter was feasible, but it would take time to organise and, more importantly, they would need to obtain permission to fly over a zone of uncertain nationality.

Hector noticed that Vayla and Not were talking to each other excitedly. Then they turned to Chief Gnar, who could speak a bit of their language because he sometimes went down to the neighbouring valleys to do business.

'I think they've found a solution,' said Jean-Marcel.

A few minutes later, Gnar went to the back of the house and returned with a small canvas pouch. After another few minutes, the professor found himself lying on his side gently sucking on a long bamboo and ivory pipe. Kneeling down beside him, Not was heating a small greyish ball on the wide-mouthed pipe bowl, and the professor, clearly soothed by this pleasant sight, breathed, or rather sighed, normally. His cheeks had gone back to their usual pink colour.

'Ah, my friends, the power of chemistry . . .' he murmured.

Hector reminded him he should try not to talk.

Hector was aware that this wonderful traditional painkiller was known to impair the breathing. And so he must make sure the benefits gained on the one hand were not lost on the other. He crouched down next to Professor Cormorant in order to monitor carefully the colour in his cheeks and the regularity of his breathing.

Chief Gnar must have misinterpreted his intentions, because Hector suddenly saw a pipe being handed to him, as well as to Jean-Marcel.

'Do you think . . .'

'This is something you don't refuse,' said Jean-Marcel, 'this is something you don't refuse.'

And the two of them found themselves lying down near the professor, whom Hector was keeping an eye on while he watched Vayla's sweet face, illuminated by the lamp's amber glow, as she prepared his pipe.

Hector is a psychiatrist, don't forget, and he was observing himself as he inhaled the sweet cloud. The professor's antidote must be a bit like this, he thought. After the first pipe, he had the impression he could enjoy Vayla's company but he wouldn't suffer if she wasn't there. After the second pipe he could think of Clara as a wonderful memory, and he wouldn't have cared whether she came back into his life or not. Vayla was about to prepare a third pipe for him, but he gestured to her not to.

He wanted to stay alert in order to watch over Professor Cormorant, who was now sleeping like a baby.

He offered his pipe to Vayla with a questioning look. She laughed, shook her head and stroked his cheek.

They went on staring into each other's eyes, while he felt love spread through him, a very serene sort of love, like blue sea under a hazy sun.

Of loving at will, of loving till death, in the land that is like you.

HECTOR AND THE FIFTH COMPONENT

AND morning came, and the forest awoke, and the sun made the dew sparkle like diamonds, and Hector saw that it was good.

He had slept as never before, after leaving the professor in Vayla and Not's care and telling them to wake him if necessary.

Vayla and Not had watched over him all night long, because he was defenceless under the influence of the drug. They themselves had drifted off to sleep only at dawn, and there they were, two sweet little doves sleeping next to the cormorant. Hector went over to make sure the professor's cheeks were still pink and that his breathing was regular.

He went back to his contemplation of the forest and then Jean-Marcel came to join him.

'Not bad, not bad,' said Jean-Marcel.

'Not something you should do every day,' said Hector.

'That's the problem. It's very easy to fall into the habit. It's just a couple of pipes every now and then, or that's what you tell yourself in any case, and then you find yourself smoking fifty a day and you weigh seven stone.'

'That doesn't seem to happen to the Gna-Doa.'

'No, but then it's part of their culture, like red wine is for us. Its use is socially controlled. If someone begins to overindulge, they deny him opium and if necessary lock him up for a while.'

'But where does the opium come from?'

'It's best not to ask that kind of question . . . You may have noticed I'm not the only one here with a satellite phone; good old Gnar has one, too,' said Jean-Marcel, smiling.

'And then it all ends up on our doorstep.'

'To be fair, we're the ones who got them growing it back in colonial times . . . It's known as a backlash.'

Hector realised that whenever he went off on a trip somewhere across the world, he encountered drugs and prostitution. Was this because they were so prevalent everywhere or because he had an unconscious attraction to those two shadowy worlds? He resolved to go and talk about it with old François when he got home. Remembering his colleague made him think of his emotive speech about love back on the island, and then immediately of Clara. He knew the opium had worn off because he felt a little stabbing pain in his heart when he thought of Clara.

'Tell me how things have improved between you and your wife,' said Hector.

'I think we've both made some progress,' said Jean-Marcel. 'She has accepted that our love has inevitably changed over time, and she no longer resents me not being the man of her dreams, like in the beginning. As for me, I've promised I'll go home. Stop spending so much time abroad. This will be my last trip, or at any rate my last long-term one.'

'Won't you miss it?'

'Yes, but everything has a price. I think I love my wife more than my trips abroad. And, you know, it might also be a question of age. I've reached a point in my life where adventures and affairs are no longer as exciting to me as they were before I turned forty. Also, it's time I saw more of my children, who are growing into adults. So, there you are.'

Hector thought of two phrases he must write in his notebook.

Seedling no. 25: Love is the ability to dream and to know when to stop dreaming.

Seedling no. 26: Love is resisting temptation.

But were we necessarily rewarded for it?

'Oh,' said Jean-Marcel, 'this came for you on the internet.'

It was a letter from old François. Hector went back to the house to read it in peace and quiet.

He sat down close to Vayla, who was still asleep.

Dear friend,

Thank you for your note on the components of heartache. I really like your categorisations and the truth of your observations. But, allow me, as your elder, to tell you that you have left out a fifth component. Adopting your system, which I have fallen for, I have set it out below.

The Fifth Component of Heartache

The fifth component is fear. Fear of eternal emptiness. The feeling that the rest of your life will be devoid of emotion now that you have lost the loved one's companionship. You realise that events or experiences which before would have moved, thrilled or saddened you now leave you cold. You have the impression that since the loved one left you, you no longer really feel anything. This is when you begin worrying about the fifth component. You wonder whether this numbing of your senses might be permanent. Naturally, you will go on working, meeting new people, experiencing new things and having affairs. You might even marry someone who is in love with you, but all this will only vaguely interest you – like those television programmes we watch because we are too lazy to decide to do something else. Your life may still be varied, but it will interest you about as much as a variety show, that's to say very little. And still you will have to endure every dull moment of it, day in day out. By now, of course, the other components of heartache will gradually have faded: you will no longer feel you need the other, just as drug addicts who haven't used for a long time no longer need their drug. Sometimes, a place, a tune, a scent will stir the memory of the loved one, you will feel a sudden rush of neediness and your friends will notice a momentary lapse in your concentration. They will have the impression from looking at your face that you are passing through an invisible cloud. Some people will understand and quickly try to distract you or lead you away, in the same way that you avoid leaving a recovering alcoholic in front of a bar for too long. In fact, you will have become like those alcoholics who manage to overcome their addiction by drinking only water, but who confess that their lives were more intense, more colourful, more fun when alcohol was their companion. You may confess to being bored with your life now, and the truth is sometimes you will make quite dull company, while still being pleasant enough. The fifth component's only advantage is that it will enable you to deal more calmly with life's everyday adversities and upsets, like a sailor who has braved the Roaring Forties and keeps his cool in a squall that would make other men tremble. So that is one reassuring thought, which you will be at pains to cultivate: what happened between you and the loved one will eventually have made you stronger and calmer, and you will even end up believing in the value of this calmness, achieved at great cost, until the moment when a place, a tune, a scent . . .

Hector understood why old François sometimes had such a melancholy air. He folded up the message and resolved not to think too much about the fifth component, which he had already felt stirring in him several times.

Then he saw Vayla wake up, looking almost surprised to find herself there, and as soon as she saw him, she smiled.

HECTOR IS FLABBERGASTED

HECTOR had brought Professor Cormorant's big metal briefcase over to him and opened it in front of him.

'It's all in here, you see,' said the professor. 'The results of all the experiments, the three-dimensional characteristics of the molecules, the thousands of pieces of compressed data. I have been careful to leave nothing lying around.'

'And what's that?' asked Hector.

He was pointing at the other half of the case, which was full of test tubes and reactive strips and looked more like a chemistry set.

'The samples,' the professor said. 'And a few little nanotechnological machines for modifying them, but you have to know how to use those.'

'What about the antidote?'

'As soon as I start feeling better I'll make some up for you; I have all the necessary components. Incidentally, how do you feel? With Vayla, I mean.'

Hector said he felt a deep attachment to Vayla and an intense desire for her, but he also felt a great need for Clara.

'At the same time?'

'No, not at the same time, it's true. When I'm in Vayla's arms, Clara recedes. But when she appears Vayla disappears.'

'Interesting, very interesting,' said Professor Cormorant. 'I would very much like to study your brain!'

This remark didn't make Hector feel any better.

The professor went on, 'To watch your brain as it consumes glucose and to see the difference between the areas that are stimulated when you think of Vayla and the ones that turn orange when you think of Clara. We would be able to distinguish anatomically between the areas associated with the different types of love! Ouch!'

In his enthusiasm, Professor Cormorant had forgotten about his fractured ribs.

'If only I had a functional MRI here,' he sighed, 'this would be the perfect place to do my research, not to mention the orang-utans!'

'What was it you gave Pelléas and Mélisande?'

'Something that creates an attachment.'

'But they're already so attached; I thought that was supposed to be their strong point.'

'Yes, they're attached to one another, but not to me.'

The professor explained that his intention had been to create in Pelléas and Mélisande a strong attachment to him, which would then have made it much easier to study them.

'But for that to work I would have had to stay with them while the product took effect, and because they ran away it failed. They will just become more attached to one another, if that's possible.'

A little further away, Vayla and Not were watching the television Chief Gnar had had brought up to the room to keep the professor amused. It ran on solar-powered batteries – Gnar certainly was a very resourceful fellow.

Suddenly, Hector heard Vayla cry out.

He approached the screen.

It showed the two pandas again, embracing each other tenderly, then a still photograph of Hi, startled by the flash, like a mug shot. Hector listened with horror to the commentary.

He saw that Vayla hadn't understood, but from the dismayed look on the presenter's face, she could tell the news contained some tragedy.

'*Noblem*?'

'Little *blem*,' he said.

'*Blem*?' she said, worried.

'*Noblem* for Vayla and Hector.'

She seemed reassured and said something to Not. Then they switched to a music channel, as though to chase away the small cloud they had felt passing over.

Hector went back over to the professor. He couldn't believe what he had just heard, and yet it was true.

'Hi has eaten Ha,' he announced.

'Really?' said Professor Cormorant, with a pensive air. 'It doesn't surprise me. That sample was adulterated, and, you know, the centres of the brain that control attachment aren't so very far from those governing appetite. In fact, the desire to eat the other in order to appropriate him or her is quite a common fantasy of people in love. In literature . . .'

'Professor Cormorant, this isn't literature! Hi ate Ha! Do you hear me! Hi ate Ha! Does this mean I am going to eat Vayla?'

Hector was getting ready to shake Professor Cormorant despite his fractured ribs, and the professor knew it.

'There's no danger of that, my friend, no danger at all!'

'Why?'

'Because . . . What I gave you two was . . . a placebo.'

HECTOR IS MOVED

JUST as Hector was trying to decide whether to shake the professor until his teeth rattled or ask him for further explanations, Jean-Marcel arrived with the translation of Vayla's letter.

Dear Hector,

At last I can speak to you, or write to you. I'm not very educated – I'm a simple girl – and I'm afraid you will be disappointed now that you can understand me. Sometimes I tell myself you prefer me to be dumb, that for you I am just a pretty doll, which you will leave, like we put away a doll when we have finished playing with it. But, at other times, I have the feeling you love me as much as I love you and that what is happening to us is a miracle. Of course, there are Kormoh's drugs, but I don't believe in all that; I don't believe I can be this much in love just because of a white professor and his magic tricks. You were different from the others. You don't know what it is to be stared at by men who sometimes only want to use you for their pleasure, Asian men as much as white men. The first time we met, when you asked me about Kormoh, I sensed you thought I was pretty, but also that you respected me and didn't take me for a girl who would roll over if you asked her to. And I noticed you didn't like it when the hotel manager who spoke English looked down his nose at me a bit, me the lowly waitress. So, you see, there are moments when I feel you are very close to me and at the same time so far away; we are worlds apart, and that makes me feel sad sometimes. I say to myself if I learn to speak your language it will bring us closer, but I also wonder whether it won't drive us apart because we come from such different worlds, and I have hardly had any education.

You are my love and you are my sorrow.

But I see our meeting as a gift, and for as long as we are together each day is a gift.

Vayla

Hector folded the letter. Vayla hadn't noticed anything and was still watching MTV Asia with Not, while Professor Cormorant carried on giving explanations which no one was listening to.

'A placebo, you understand, was a way of making the experiment a little more rigorous, of finding out exactly what could be attributed to the product, the real product, the one Not and I took. But we need more subjects. And a functional MRI, of course.'

Hector wasn't paying attention to him. He was watching Vayla and the expression of childlike wonder on her face as she looked at the image of Madonna singing in English again as she walked along a glittering pathway strewn with rose petals.

And each day with you is a gift.

'I hope everything is all right,' said Jean-Marcel. 'I printed it, but I didn't read it.'

'Things aren't bad,' said Hector.

'I don't know – you look worried.'

'You're right, I shouldn't spoil my own happiness.'

He was about to go over to Vayla to take her to their house and show her he had read her letter, when the sound of an engine came over the horizon.

Everybody rushed to look up at the sky.

The noise grew louder, and then a helicopter appeared from behind a distant hill.

'It's a big one,' said Jean-Marcel. 'An army helicopter.'

The village was suddenly the centre of a huge commotion; the women ran indoors with their children while a number of men disappeared into the forest, some of them weighed down by heavy jute bags on their backs.

The helicopter was drawing closer, like a big khaki-coloured bee, and the flag of one of the neighbouring countries was clearly marked on the side of the cabin.

'One thing's for sure, this is not a police operation,' said Jean-Marcel. 'They would have put down at a distance.'

The helicopter approached a small clearing near the paddy fields, causing the buffaloes to panic and hurl themselves, bellowing, against the gate of their enclosure. The helicopter wobbled slightly as it approached the ground then landed gently. The two pilots were in army uniforms. The cabin door opened and two quite young-looking Westerners in suits appeared first, followed by a couple.

Clara and Gunther.

Professor Cormorant had dragged himself over to the doorway to watch.

'Not him,' he said. 'Don't let him take it!'

Hector and Jean-Marcel looked at one another.

HECTOR CONTROLS HIMSELF

'WELL,' said Gunther, 'we have some common interests so we need to reach an agreement.'

Everyone was sitting cross-legged in a circle around Professor Cormorant, like a little group of courtiers gathered round an ailing king: Hector, Gunther and his two colleagues, who looked as healthy and clean-cut as a couple of astronauts in civvies and answered to the names Derek and Ralph. And Clara, of course, dressed in a very attractive safari outfit straight out of a women's glossy magazine, and avoiding Hector's eyes. Not was holding the professor's hand and fanning him, and Chief Gnar, who sensed there was possible business to be done, was also there, as well as Aang-long-arms, who could understand a bit of English. And what about Jean-Marcel?

Jean-Marcel had disappeared before Gunther arrived. Nearby, Vayla went on watching television, or rather pretending to, while shooting sidelong glances at Hector and at Clara.

'Couldn't she turn the volume down a bit?' asked Gunther. 'We are here to work.'

One of the young men, Ralph, started to get up to go over and have a word with Vayla, but Hector stopped him, saying, 'No, leave it.'

Ralph sat back down because he sensed from Hector's tone that this was about something more than just the noise of a television.

'Will the professor pull through?' Derek asked, looking concerned.

Actually, despite Not's attentions, Professor Cormorant had taken a sudden turn for the worse since Gunther had arrived. Eyes closed and looking pale, he was breathing very weakly.

'He has a couple of broken ribs,' said Hector, 'and only one lung.'

'Precisely,' said Gunther. 'We can take him back with us. There's an excellent clinic an hour from here by helicopter.'

'Out of the question . . .' murmured the professor. 'I'm staying with my friends. My research . . . The orang-utans . . .'

'What did you say?' asked Gunther. 'Is he delirious?'

'Not at all. Professor Cormorant wants to study the orang-utans. To understand why they are monogamous.'

'Very well,' said Gunther, 'we could set up a research station for you. We could use the helicopter to transport the necessary equipment.'

'A functional MRI,' whispered Professor Cormorant.

At this, Gunther pulled a face. 'Really? But wouldn't it be better to set that up in town? What about electricity?'

'Electricity very good!' exclaimed Chief Gnar. 'Electricity very good, if you bring generator!'

Gunther seemed surprised by the chief's sudden intervention.

Gnar went on excitedly, 'Generator, solar-powered batteries, turbine for river! Always strong current! Very, very good! Helicopter bring all this!'

'Well, the chief seems to know what he's talking about,' Derek said to Gunther.

'Equipment for my experiments . . .' the professor continued. 'Chromatograph, synthesiser, etc.'

'Equipment very good! Helicopter bring all this!'

'Aang set equipment up,' said Aang, joining in his chief's enthusiasm.

Gunther looked at Clara, but Clara's eyes were fixed on Vayla. Gunther felt his heart sink. My God, he thought, I'm so vulnerable! And yet this isn't the right moment.

'Professor,' he said, 'these projects are all very interesting. But what about your recent results, your samples? Where are they?'

The professor made a vague gesture with his hand in the direction of the door, and beyond, to the forest and the mountains.

'We've put them somewhere safe,' said Hector.

'Somewhere safe?' Gunther's broad face had suddenly gone pink.

'There are too many people interested in the research,' continued Hector. 'The Chinese, the Japanese . . . The professor and I decided to put the professor's results in a safe place.'

'And you are going to take us there, of course.'

'No,' said Hector.

This time Gunther turned pale.

'We paid for this research, it belongs to us,' he said through gritted teeth.

Derek and Ralph looked at one another uneasily; they had already seen Gunther lose his temper. Gnar and Aang also seemed very attentive and had straightened up slightly, as though ready to jump up.

Hector was delighted. He wished Gunther would fly at him so he could punch him in the face, which shows that psychiatrists are just like other men.

'Look,' said Clara, 'I think we all need to calm down.'

Seeing her so calm and self-possessed, her voice as sweet-sounding as it would be if she were chairing an ordinary meeting, Hector felt admiration and, it has to be said, love for Clara. When he saw the way Gunther, who had also calmed down, was looking at her, he said to himself: God, that bastard loves her. And that made him feel on the one hand panic, because he could be sure Gunther would do everything in his power to keep her, and on the other relief, because the thought of Clara suffering at the hands of a man who didn't love her was so dreadful it made him feel homicidal. Strangely, at that moment he had an almost brotherly feeling towards Gunther, a curious sense of being sort of in the same boat on a rough sea, but at the same time thinking they could each try to throw the other overboard.

Vayla had stopped watching television and come to sit down closer to them, just behind him. He sensed she was also looking at Clara.

'So,' Clara said, a slight catch in her voice, 'what exactly are your demands? You clearly have something in mind.'

Hector explained that Professor Cormorant was worried that his research, which he considered incomplete, would be put to premature use. He didn't want a faulty drug to be released onto the market.

'But we would never do that,' said Gunther. 'It isn't in our interests!'

'It's not only up to you,' whispered the professor. 'I want to be in complete control of what I do. I don't want other research teams working on this project.'

Then he seemed to fall asleep. Gunther didn't reply. Hector was beginning to see why Professor Cormorant had gone on the run.

'So Professor Cormorant wants to continue his research here. In peace and quiet,' he confirmed.

The professor's lips suddenly began to move, as if he were talking in his sleep.

'I want a functional MRI set up here in the village,' said Professor Cormorant, 'and freedom to use the helicopter whenever necessary.'

Gunther thought for a moment. Clara looked at Hector, her eyes glistening, and he, too, suddenly felt close to tears. He told himself they were both tormented by jealousy, he at seeing Gunther and she at seeing Vayla, but this wasn't enough to show they still loved each other. He resolved to write in his notebook: *Jealousy can outlast love. But is it still love?*

Gunther did what he was good at: he took a decision.

'All right. You'll be free to stay on here. But I need a guarantee, something I can take back to company headquarters, to show them we are making progress. I need some samples!'

Professor Cormorant didn't reply, as though Gunther bored him so much he had fallen asleep.

Gunther's face flushed. 'And if I don't get them, *niet* to everything! And I'll send an army to raze this village and the surrounding jungle.'

Just then, they heard the long-drawn-out *ou-ou* of the orang-utan coming from outside. Hector said to himself this was the signal for them to conclude the agreement. He was beginning to think like a Gna-Doa.

HECTOR IS TRICKED

HECTOR was walking through the jungle behind Aang-long-arms. In the middle of the clearing frequented by Pelléas and Mélisande, who were out for a stroll, they found Jean-Marcel, sitting on the professor's steel briefcase.

'So what's the news?'

'The professor is free to stay on here, in exchange for a few samples.'

'That's a good deal,' said Jean-Marcel. 'Well done.'

'I think Gunther wants to get away from here as soon as possible. That must have helped.'

'What an idiot! It's so amazing here.'

The effects of the opium had worn off, but Jean-Marcel seemed much calmer than Hector had ever seen him.

'Those mountains . . . this forest,' he said, gesturing with a wide sweep of his hand towards the landscape. 'The friendly people . . . I could easily imagine living here, in one of those houses. The good life, you know. Hunting, fishing . . . a little pipe from time to time. I'd ask Gnar to find me a wife . . . The local women are very nice.'

'What about your wife?'

Jean-Marcel jumped.

'For God's sake, have you no imagination? I was daydreaming. Well, then, which samples are we giving those bastards?'

'The professor said all the ones with labels beginning CC and WW.'

They opened the briefcase and began examining the test tubes, arranged in neat rows like ammunition.

'Step aside,' a voice behind them said.

Derek and Ralph had come up behind them, accompanied by four young Asian soldiers. Despite their camouflage clothing and the ease with which they handled their weapons, they seemed quite uncomfortable pointing their guns at two white men, even under the orders of other white men.

'Damn,' said Jean-Marcel. 'What gives you the right?'

'Just don't try anything stupid and everything will be all right,' said Derek. 'We only want the briefcase.'

Aang-long-arms stood motionless, but Hector could feel his anger mounting.

'It's all right, Aang,' he said, placing his hand on Aang's shoulder.

He realised that shooting someone like Aang would have been no problem for the young soldiers.

'Finally, we get back our investment,' said Ralph, walking over to the open briefcase.

'But what are you going to do with it? Cormorant will refuse to carry on working.'

'Do you really imagine we want to carry on working with that old lunatic? He's caused us enough trouble already. Granted, he's a genius, but now we need reliable researchers. This will give them plenty to get on with,' said Ralph, closing the briefcase and going back over to the soldiers.

Hector understood this had been Gunther's intention from the start. The negotiations had been a sham, to make him lead them to the samples. He suddenly felt as furious as Aang.

'Calm down,' said Jean-Marcel. 'Don't do anything stupid.'

'Stop whispering,' said Derek. 'All right, we're going to make our way back slowly. Don't follow us too closely – the soldiers are jumpy here; it's not their favourite place from what I've heard. If I were you, I'd keep well behind.'

He walked a few paces then turned round. 'Better still, stay here until you hear the helicopter engine start.'

Hector had a sudden realisation, as painful as if he'd been hit with a club. The samples. Gunther would have at his disposal the real drug, the one the professor had perfected, not the placebo. Clara. Clara and Gunther.

HECTOR LOSES HIS TEMPER

HECTOR was running. He could hear Aang's footsteps behind him, and further away those of Jean-Marcel. He had one sole aim, to reach the village before Derek and his group. He tore down a forest slope, parallel to the one the others were on. Hector had no clear plan as yet, but he told himself it couldn't be that difficult to stop a helicopter from taking off.

'Technically speaking, there's nothing to stop us from trying,' Jean-Marcel had told him. 'But there are the two pilots, who are no doubt also armed.'

'What if you use your rifle?'

Jean-Marcel had paused. 'That's for defending myself, or you. Not to confront soldiers whose country isn't at war with ours.'

'Do you think they are real soldiers?'

'They're moonlighting, like everyone here. Anyway, we wouldn't stand a chance.'

And so Hector had carried on running, consumed by the image of Gunther in a dinner jacket at a table outside Danieli's as the sun set over Venice, Clara with her back to him, splendid in a black evening dress, watching the golden light fade on the Grand Canal, while Gunther, laughing gleefully, emptied the contents of a phial into her glass of champagne.

They arrived at the edge of the village, which was still deserted. They saw the two pilots smoking next to the helicopter. Two isn't very many, Hector thought, maybe with the Gna-Doas' help . . . He ran up the ladder to find Chief Gnar, followed by Aang-long-arms.

They were all still there: the professor lying down, Not by his side, and then Gunther, Clara and the chief, who was drinking tea, and at a slight distance Vayla, who gave a shriek of joy when she saw him arrive.

'You bastard!' said Hector. 'You've stolen the briefcase!'

Gunther looked at him calmly. 'You can't steal what's already yours.'

'All that negotiating was just a trick . . .'

'That's business,' Gunther said with a shrug.

'How can you be with such a bastard!' Hector said to Clara.

'Leave her out of this!' said Gunther.

'I'm not talking to you, you big oaf,' said Hector.

'You should reread your contract, you poor fool,' said Gunther.

'You see,' Hector said to Clara, 'that's exactly what I mean.'

At this, Gunther began to get angry and he stood up.

HECTOR RECEIVES A LESSON IN GNA-DOA WISDOM

GNAR and Aang finally pulled them apart.

Hector felt the blood trickle from his nose, and at the same time he noticed with glee that a missing tooth would give Gunther's smile a rather loutish look for the time being. (Though right now he wasn't smiling at all.)

'God!' said Gunther, who had just that moment noticed it himself.

The chief and Aang were still keeping them apart, a look of surprise and vague admiration on their faces. It turned out these strange, reserved white men were capable of exchanging blows like real men.

Vayla had rushed over and was trying to staunch the flow of blood from Hector's nose with a piece of cloth while giving little sympathetic sighs. But what he saw next caused him far more pain than his possible broken nose: Clara had rushed over to Gunther and was examining his split lip. That says it all, he thought.

'Thith ithn't over yet, you bathtard,' Gunther went on in a furious voice.

'You bet it isn't!' said Hector, straightening up.

This rush of hatred felt so good he wondered why he always tried to encourage his patients to control it. The chief and Aang stood between them again.

But once Hector had sat down and put his head back to stop the bleeding he saw Clara's face appear next to

Vayla's. The two women exchanged a look of simultaneous incomprehension and knowing – we realise men are crazy – then looked at him, concerned. And for a moment, beneath their gazes, so similar and yet so different, he felt incredibly happy. The memory of a paradise lost, or a sultan's daydream, he thought.

And then, certain he wasn't badly hurt, Clara went away. He heard her murmuring words of comfort to Gunther.

Suddenly Hector felt ashamed. Fighting. So, after all, he and Gunther had behaved just like the crabs he had seen fighting on the island. Another consequence of love: it reduced you to the level of your friends the crabs. Of course you might think the reason for the fight was the theft of the briefcase, but he and Gunther knew that wasn't true.

'Will somebody tell me what's going on?' said Professor Cormorant angrily. 'Where's my briefcase?'

Not had taken him over to a corner of the room, afraid the brawling men might fall on her beloved Kormoh.

'Gunther had Ralph and the other guy and some soldiers steal your briefcase.'

'Is that true? Is that true?'

'What did you think?' said Gunther, running his tongue painfully around the inside of his mouth. 'That we'd go on working with a maniac like you?'

'But it's my research!' Professor Cormorant cried out, suddenly sitting up straight. His cheeks were pink and he looked wide awake. 'And anyway you can't do anything without me!'

Gunther sniggered. 'The cry of the geniuth . . .'

But one look from Clara and he stopped short.

'Profethor Cormorant, you've done very good work, brilliant work, even . . . But now it'th time to begin working theriously.'

'Who do you think will agree to work under these conditions if I won't, for God's sake?'

Gunther said nothing, as though it posed no problem.

Professor Cormorant was struck by a sudden realisation. 'Rupert? You're going to get that bastard Rupert to work on this?'

The professor had leapt to his feet, and Hector thought he was going to hurl himself at Gunther, but the chief and Aang intervened again.

'No problem,' the chief said, 'no problem.'

'No problem,' Aang repeated.

'Yes,' said Hector, 'big problem.'

The chief smiled and drew his attention to the scenery outside. Was the chief implying that contemplating nature was the most important thing and that all man's petty disputes were in vain?

Hector saw a small group of Gna-Doas appear at the edge of the forest. They must be returning from the hunt because they seemed to be carrying heavy trophies tied to long poles resting on their shoulders.

Then he made out Derek, Ralph and the four soldiers, suspended by their hands and feet, like hammocks. And where the helicopter was, there were no pilots in sight, just a group of Gna-Doas guffawing loudly.

HECTOR WINS

'WHAT a useless bunch,' said Jean-Marcel. 'Another example of bad recruiting! Bringing along conscripts with no fighting experience. They should have got some real soldiers, or other mountain people, but to do that you need contacts!'

Jean-Marcel seemed be enjoying himself analysing the failure of Ralph and Derek's great operation.

'. . . those inexperienced rookies, useless without a rule book to follow,' he said. 'And they thought they could get away with it in the middle of Gna-Doa territory! Where people have been engaging in guerrilla warfare for generations! Well, it's lucky we were here, otherwise I reckon those young lads would have ended up on an anthill, and that would have been the last anyone heard of them . . . The Gna-Doas have always had problems with people in authority.'

Hector and Jean-Marcel were drinking tea with Chief Gnar and using the briefcase between them as a table, a real symbol of their victory, a bit like drinking out of their enemies' skulls, only nicer.

Gunther, Derek, Ralph, the pilots and the soldiers were locked in the pigsty. Hector had thought this a bit harsh, but Jean-Marcel had explained that it really was the minimum penalty for entering Gna-Doa territory armed.

Ralph and Derek's plan had been doomed to failure the moment some of the village children saw the four soldiers slip out of the helicopter and disappear into the forest. And perhaps the boy or girl who had raised the alarm was at that very moment playing around them, and laughing the way children do, because they were very happy at being allowed to stay around the important grown-ups, so happy they were doing somersaults.

Professor Cormorant appeared next to them, a little unsteady on his feet but sturdy all the same.

'The problem is,' he said, 'I'll always be afraid they are going to try to steal everything off me again. I shall have to go away again with my sweet Not.'

Not and Vayla were talking, watched by Clara, who had escaped being shut in with the pigs thanks to Hector's intervention. She was sitting quietly on the floor in the furthest corner of the room. Hector was longing to go and speak to her, but he didn't want to do it in front of all these people – he would be too afraid they might fall into each other's arms, and he was thinking of Vayla.

Footsteps vibrated on the ladder outside and Miko and Chizourou appeared, a little embarrassed at first, then increasingly interested in Professor Cormorant's briefcase. Chief Gnar welcomed them with open arms then pointed to the women's corner, where Vayla and Not were already sitting, because there really was no reason to get carried away.

'It's a pity,' said Professor Cormorant, 'I'm sure Pelléas and Mélisande were starting to get used to me.'

'And how are you planning to leave?' asked Jean-Marcel.

'You could drive me to town in your car. From there, I'm sure I'll find a plane going somewhere. Or even a train – apparently there's an old colonial railway route that's very picturesque. I'm sure Not will like that.'

Hector thought Not would almost certainly prefer to go to Shanghai than to some other remote village in the jungle.

'What about the others?'

'Oh,' said Jean-Marcel, 'they'll let them go. The chief knows he can't poach or even ransom big game like Gunther. Isn't that right, Chief?'

And Chief Gnar began to chuckle, either because he agreed with Jean-Marcel, or because he always felt cheerful after a victory, or for some other reason only he knew about.

'We could celebrate with something a bit stronger than tea,' Jean-Marcel suggested, making good old Chief Gnar laugh even louder.

Hector went on pretending to take part in the conversation when in fact all he wanted was to talk to Clara.

HECTOR AND CLARA AND VAYLA

LATER on, Hector found Clara outside, at the foot of the ladder. She had come back from seeing Gunther, or rather from talking to him through the door of the pig pen guarded by two armed Gna-Doas.

'Let's have a talk,' he said.

It was getting dark and he could sense that, like the Gna-Doa women, Clara didn't like being outside here at night. They could hear Jean-Marcel and the chief laughing above their heads, and Professor Cormorant, who had discovered the joys of fermented rice wine and possibly *choum-choum*.

'About what?' said Clara mournfully.

'Can you think of anything?'

Clara didn't reply, but she pressed her forehead against Hector's shoulder, like a stubborn little bull that knows this is life and there is nothing to do but to face it head on.

'I think we still love each other,' said Hector.

'And we always will,' said Clara.

There was a silence. Hector waited.

'But it's impossible now . . .'

Above them, Hector glimpsed Vayla's face peering into the darkness and he thought she might see them. He stepped back to move away from Clara.

'You see . . .' Clara said.

*

During the night, Hector couldn't sleep. He could feel Vayla's restless breathing close to him. He was thinking about those who say it is impossible to love two people at the same time, who say that that isn't true love. And yet he had often come across such stories through his patients; and it was not only the case for men, which was nothing new, but also for women, which was less talked about. And now here he was experiencing it himself, like in *Doctor Zhivago*, a film that had left a deep impression on him. You had to choose between your two loves so that you did not destroy them both. He resolved to write down:

Seedling no 27: You can only have one love at a time.

But perhaps that was too much like *Love is resisting temptation*. He fell asleep.

He felt Vayla's face close to his, her breath on his cheek. He wanted to put his arms around her, but he saw she looked worried and wanted him to wake up.

'*Blem*,' she whispered, gesturing towards the doorway, which was open to the outside.

Dawn was beginning to colour the sky, but the village was still in darkness. Vayla pointed to the chief's house where Jean-Marcel and Professor Cormorant had stayed overnight. Hector heard a faint rustling, and, given the turn the evening had taken, it would have been surprising if his friends had woken up this early.

'*Blem!*' whispered Vayla, frowning.

Two small figures had begun descending the ladder of the chief's house. One of them was holding something that shone for a second in the pale dawn light. The professor's briefcase. Miko and Chizourou were stealing away with his briefcase.

HECTOR SAVES LOVE

LATER, as he was running through the dark forest, he said to himself that Japanese martial arts were truly formidable, but that body weight and long legs were still decisive advantages. His nose had started bleeding again, he wondered whether one of his ribs wasn't broken and the weight of the briefcase was pulling on his arm, but he felt as if he had wings.

Of course, the noise of him running might alert a tiger, but somehow he couldn't quite believe it.

He stopped. No sound behind him. He had shaken off the two pretty and formidable young Japanese women. He continued on his way, walking this time and catching his breath.

The trees thinned out around him and suddenly he found himself at the edge of a cliff, overlooking a vast wooded plain stretching as far as the eye could see. In the distance, the ruins of a temple seemed to be waking up with the sun's first rays.

At his feet, a hundred yards below, a fast mountain stream flowed.

Facing the rising sun, Hector deliberated. The briefcase contained the promise of a solution for all those who suffered as a result of love – spurned love, loving too much, a lack of love, the death of love, as old François had said. But he also remembered Hi and Ha and Dr Wei and Miko and Chizourou, and how afraid he had felt when he thought of the ways in which Gunther or others might use the professor's research. To create forced enslavement. To compel people to form attachments, even a victim to his executioner.

Love was complicated, love was painful, love was the cause of so much unhappiness.

'But love is freedom!' he said out loud.

And Hector threw the briefcase into the fast-moving stream.

HECTOR HAS A DREAM

THAT night, with Vayla's breath on his neck, Hector had a dream.

He was standing at the top of a beautiful Chinese mountain, in the company of an old monk he had met on his last big trip. The monk was carefully reading a text on the five components of heartache that Hector had brought him. They were surrounded by sun and clouds, and by the wind that rustled the pages in the monk's hands. When he had finished reading, he smiled.

'It's good,' he said, 'but here you only talk about the dark side of love.'

'How do I talk about the bright side?'

'They are the same!' said the old monk. And he laughed.

And suddenly everything became clear to Hector. Five components versus five components.

First component of love: fulfilment (the other side of neediness), the simple happiness of being with the loved one, the feeling of calm when the loved one laughs, sleeps, thinks, the incomparable happiness of simply being in each other's arms.

Hector had experienced this feeling with Clara. And, it had to be said, with Vayla.

Second component: the joy of giving (the other side of guilt), feeling happy because we make others happy, saying to ourselves that with us the loved one has experienced joys they would not have experienced without us, that we have brought new light into their life, in the same way they have brought new light into ours.

Hector remembered this was similar to one of the lessons he had learnt from the old monk during his first trip: happiness is caring about the happiness of those you love.

Third component: gratitude (the other side of anger), being amazed by what we owe the loved one, the joy they have given us, the way they have helped us mature, the way they have been able to comfort and understand us, and to share our pleasures and sorrows.

Hector remembered what Clara had said to him one day: 'Thank you for existing.' And he also remembered Vayla's letter.

Fourth component: self-confidence (the other side of low self-esteem), feeling happy to be who we are simply because the loved one loves us for who we are, with all our strengths and weaknesses. Despite our ordeals and setbacks, the criticism of others, and the cruelty of life, feeling a measure of self-confidence thanks to what really matters to us: being loved by the loved one.

Hector thought of all the people he had helped, but he knew he had only been able to do it because someone else still loved them no matter what.

Fifth component: serenity (the other side of fear), knowing that, despite life's ups and downs and its inevitable tragic end, the loved one will be with us on this journey. The tests of time, illness, all of this will be bearable with the loved one by our side, for better or for worse, in happiness as in adversity.

Hector was still too young to give much thought to this component, but watching the smiling old monk he remembered how important it was.

Later, he sent the five components of love to old François, thinking they would do him good, provided, of course, they didn't make him even sadder.

EPILOGUE

AND how did the whole story end? you are going to ask.

Hector had thrown away all Professor Cormorant's research and that can't have made everyone happy. So what happened to him?

Of course, Gunther threatened to sue him for vast sums of money, but then Hector threatened to reveal the true story about Hi and Ha, and that put a stop to that. Gunther's company spent hundreds of millions of dollars on publicity in order to give the impression of being an organisation with the best interests of health and the environment at heart. He didn't want to become known as the man who had employed a mad genius who transformed a nice panda into a cannibalistic lover.

Professor Cormorant disappeared again with the gentle Not, and you can expect our dear eccentric to pull other marvels or horrors out of his hat one day. And if he doesn't, others will, because plenty of people are interested in the mechanisms of love and they have no lack of funds, so begin rejoicing or worrying. Of course, the professor is very annoyed with Hector since the business with the briefcase, and it will be some time before they get in touch again, but you can be sure they will.

Jean-Marcel went back to live with his wife and children, carrying on his job as a businessman only and travelling much less. They are happy, and they also know they need to work at staying happy.

Of course, Jean-Marcel was also upset with Hector for throwing away the briefcase. What's more, he didn't speak to him on their way back from the Gna-Doa village. But when they arrived, and it was time to say goodbye at the airport, Jean-Marcel whispered to him, 'I shouldn't say this to you, but I probably would have done exactly the same as you.'

And they parted the best of friends.

Miko and Chizourou went back to Japan, which is only natural. And, incidentally, the marriage rate in Japan has begun to pick up again in the last few months, if you are following events. Miko and Chizourou still got to work with Professor Cormorant for a while, as Lee and Wu.

The Gna-Doas carried on living the way they have always lived, that is, quite happily when nobody wages war on them. If you go there, you will understand, especially when you hear their children laughing.

Pelléas and Mélisande are still around, and the professor was on the right track with his research, because Pelléas has never eaten Mélisande and they seem more attached to each other than ever.

Captain Lin Zaou of the People's Liberation Army . . .

Hold on, you're going to say, we couldn't care less about her. We want to know what happened to Hector and Vayla, and to Clara and Gunther, that's what we really want to know about!

Well, that's the problem – we don't really know.

Some people will tell you the whole story was a rumour and that Hector and Clara are still together, that they may have had problems, like every couple, but they were able to deal with them and are now thinking of having a baby, while Gunther continues to be a loving father and husband to his wife and daughter, who incidentally is doing better.

Other people will tell you this is not what happened at all and you are completely mistaken. Because they have it on good authority that Hector is living with Vayla over there in the mountains, in a house on stilts. And sometimes you see them together in the town with all the temples when they go to do their shopping, and Hector comes to collect money and medicines for the clinic he has set up in one of the Gna-Doa villages. Hector and Vayla are also thinking of having a baby. Hector and Clara still keep in touch over the internet because they will always love each other, even though they now feel a different kind of love for someone else, and both Vayla and Gunther understand that.

Stuff and nonsense, others will tell you. Hector was so exhausted after his latest adventures in Asia he decided to withdraw from the world and its temptations, and he has gone on a retreat for a while to a monastery in China, the same one where the old monk he met during his first trip lives.

So who are you to believe? You could always try to find out, but the problem is still more people will tell you all these stories are true, or at any rate they all happened, in the real world, or in some other world, no less real.

Because love is indeed complicated, difficult, sometimes painful, but it is also the only time that our dream becomes reality, as old François used to say.

ACKNOWLEDGEMENTS

I would like to thank the friends that accompanied Hector on his travels, and introduced him to new horizons. Of those I am able to mention, I would particularly like to thank: Nicolas Audier, Jean-Michel Caldagues, Peer De Jong, Patrick de Kouzmine Karavaieff and Olivia Chai, Perr De Jong, Franck Lafourcade, Lin Menuhin and Xia Qing, Jean-Jacques Muletier, Yves Nicolaï, Servane Rangheard and, of course, Étienne Aubert, for her talents as a crooner.

My thanks to Odile Jacob and Bernard Gotlieb, and to their respective teams for their renewed help and support throughout Hector's second adventure.

Hector and other characters quoted extracts of the following works: *Phèdre* by Jean Racine, 'Love' by Nat King Cole, 'Lullaby' by W. H. Auden, 'L'Invitation au voyage' by Charles Baudelaire.

And thank you to Georges Condominas for his book *Nous avons mangé la forêt* (Mercure de France).

Read on for the opening chapters of
François Lelord's third novel
about Hector

Hector and
the Search for Lost Time

Coming from Penguin in
2012

THE first time Sabine came to see Hector it was because she was getting upset at work. Sabine worked in an office, and her boss wasn't nice to her: he often made her cry. Of course, she always cried in private, but even so, it was terribly hard for her.

Little by little, Hector helped her realise that perhaps she deserved better than a boss who was not nice to her and Sabine built up enough self-confidence to find a new job. And these days, she was happier.

Gradually Hector had changed the way he worked. In the beginning, he mainly tried to help people to change their outlook. Now, he still did that, of course, but he also helped people to change their lives, to find a new life which would suit them better. Because, to put it another way, if you're a cow, you'll never become a horse, even with a good psychiatrist. It's better to find a nice meadow where people need milk than to try to gallop around a racecourse. And, above all, it's best to avoid entering a bullring, because that's always a disaster.

Sabine would not have been happy being compared to a cow, even though cows are actually kind and gentle animals, Hector had always thought, and very good mothers too. It is true that she was also very clever, and sometimes this did not make her happy, because, as you might already have noticed, sometimes happiness is not knowing the whole story.

One day, Sabine said to Hector, 'Sometimes, I think life is just a big con.'

Startled, Hector asked, 'What do you mean?' (That was what he always said when he hadn't been listening properly the first time).

'Well, you're born, and before you know it, you have to rush about, going to school, then work, having children, and then your parents die and then . . . you get old and die too.'

'This all takes a bit of time, though, doesn't it?'

'Yes, but it goes by so quickly. Especially when there's no time to stop. Take me, for example, work, children, husband . . . He's the same, poor guy – he never stops either.'

Sabine had a nice husband (she had also had a nice father, which straight away improves the chances of finding a nice husband), who worked hard in an office too. And two young children, the eldest of whom had started school.

'I always feel like I'm up against the clock,' said Sabine. 'In the morning, everything needs to be organised, we have to leave in time to take my eldest to school, and then dash to the office. There are meetings, which you have to be on time for, but while you're there, the rest of your work piles up, and then you have to rush in the evenings too, to pick up your child from school, or get home in time for the nanny, and then dinner, and homework . . . Still,

I'm lucky, my husband helps me. We hardly have time to speak to each other in the evening: we're so tired, we both just fall asleep.'

Hector knew all this, and perhaps that was partly why he had spent a lot of time thinking about, considering, contemplating whether to give serious thought to marrying and having babies.

'I'd like time to slow down,' said Sabine. 'I'd like to have time to enjoy life. I'd like some time for myself, to do whatever I want.'

'What about holidays?' asked Hector.

Sabine smiled.

'You don't have children, do you, Doctor?'

Hector admitted that he did not, not yet.

'Actually,' said Sabine, 'I think that's also why I come to see you. This session is the only point in my week when time stops, when my time is completely my own.'

Hector understood precisely what Sabine meant. Especially since he, too, over the course of his day, often felt that he was up against the clock, like all of his colleagues. When you are a psychiatrist, you always have to pay attention to the time, because if you allow your patient to talk to you for too long, the next patient will become impatient in the waiting room. Then all your appointments will run late that day. (Sometimes, this was very difficult for Hector – for example, when three minutes before the end of a session, just as he began to shift in his armchair to signal that time was almost up, the patient with him would suddenly say, 'Deep down, Doctor, I think my mother never loved me,' and start to cry.)

Being up against the clock was a real problem for so many people, especially for mums, thought Hector. What could he possibly do to help them?

HECTOR AND THE MAN WHO LOVED DOGS

HECTOR had another patient, a man called Fernand, who was not particularly remarkable, except for the fact that he had no friends. And he didn't have a wife or girlfriend either. Was it because he had a very monotonous voice, or because he looked a little like a heron? Hector didn't know, but he thought it very unfair that Fernand didn't have any friends, since he was nice and said things that were very interesting (although slightly odd, it has to be admitted).

One day, out of the blue, Fernand said to Hector, 'Anyway, Doctor, at my age, I've got no more than two and a half dogs left.'

'Sorry?' said Hector.

He remembered that Fernand had a dog (one day, Fernand had brought one with him, a very well-behaved dog that had slept throughout their session), but not two, and he couldn't even begin to imagine what half a dog might be.

'Well,' said Fernand, 'a dog lives for fourteen or fifteen years, doesn't it?'

Hector then realised that Fernand was measuring the time he had left in the number of dogs he would have over the rest of his life. As a result, Hector set about measuring the rest of his life in dog lives (that is, which he probably had left, for ye know neither the day nor the hour, as somebody who died quite young once said), and he wasn't sure if it would be three or four. Of course, he thought to himself, this number could change if science made incredible advances to make you live longer, but perhaps on the other hand it wouldn't, since scientists would no doubt make dogs live longer too, which, you can be sure, no one would ask their opinion about.

Hector spoke to his friends about this method of measuring your life in dogs, and they were absolutely horrified.

'How awful!'

'Not only that, thinking of your dog dying . . . it's too sad for words.'

'Exactly. That's why I just couldn't have another, because when our little Darius died, it was far too upsetting.'

'You really do see some complete loonies!'

'Measuring time in dogs?! And why not in cats or parrots?'

'And if he had a cow, would he measure it in cows?'

Listening to all his friends talking about Fernand's idea, it dawned on Hector that what they did not like about it at all was this: measuring your life in dogs makes it seem shorter. Two, three, four dogs, even five, doesn't make it sound as if you're here for very long!

He understood better why Fernand unnerved people a bit with his way of seeing things. If Fernand had measured his life in canaries or goldfish, would he have had more friends?

In his own lonely and odd little way, Fernand had put his finger on a real problem with time. For that matter, lots of poets had been talking about it forever, and Sabine had too.

They said . . . the years fly by, time is fleeting, and time goes by too quickly.

HECTOR AND THE LITTLE BOY WHO WANTED TO SPEED UP TIME

EVERY so often children also came to see Hector, and when they did, of course it was their parents who had decided to send them.

The children who came to see Hector weren't really ill – it was more that their parents found them difficult to understand, or else they were children who were too sad, too fearful or too worked-up. One day, he talked to a little boy who, funnily enough, was called Hector, just like him. Little Hector was very bored at school, and time seemed to go by too slowly for him. So he didn't listen, and he ended up with bad marks.

Grown-up Hector asked Little Hector, 'Right now, what do you wish for most in the world?'

Little Hector didn't hesitate for a second. 'To become a grown-up straight away!'

Hector was surprised. He had expected Little Hector's answer to be: 'For my parents to get back together', or 'To get better marks at school', or 'To go on a school ski trip with my friends'.

So he asked Little Hector why he wanted to become a grown-up straight away.

'To decide things!' said Little Hector.

If he became a grown-up straight away, explained Little Hector, he could decide for himself what time to go to bed, when to wake up, and where he could spend his holidays. He could see the friends he wanted, have fun doing what he wanted, and not see grown-ups he didn't want to see (like his dad's new girlfriend). He would also have a real job, because going to school wasn't a real job. Besides, you don't choose to go to school, and then you spend hours, days, years watching time going by slowly and getting bored.

Hector thought that Little Hector had let his imagination run away with him about life as a grown-up: after all, grown-ups still had to do things they didn't like doing, and see people they didn't like seeing. But he didn't tell Little Hector that, because he thought that, for the moment, it was a good thing that Little Hector was dreaming of a happy future, since his present was decidedly less so.

So he asked Little Hector, 'But if you became a grown-up straight away, it would mean that you would already have lived for a good few years, and then you'd have fewer left to live. Wouldn't that bother you?'

Little Hector thought it over. 'Okay, it's a bit like a video game when you lose an extra life. It's annoying, but it doesn't stop you having fun!'

Then he looked at Hector. 'What about you? Would it bother you to have already lost one or two lives?'

Grown-up Hector thought that Little Hector might become a psychiatrist himself one day.

HECTOR THINKS THINGS OVER

AT the end of each day, Hector thought about all the people he'd listened to who were worried about time.

He thought about Sabine, who wanted to slow time down.

He thought about Fernand, who measured his life in dogs.

He thought about Little Hector, who wanted to speed time up.

And many others . . .

Hector spent more and more time thinking about time.

AVAILABLE FROM PENGUIN

ISBN 978-0-14-311839-8

The first novel in François Lelord's internationally bestselling series, *Hector and the Search for Happiness* follows the young psychiatrist as he travels from Paris to China to Africa to the United States, hoping to find the secret to happiness. Combining the winsome appeal of *The Little Prince* with the inspiring philosophy of *The Alchemist*, Hector's journey around the world and into the human soul is entertaining, empowering, and smile-inducing—as winning in its optimism as it is wise in its simplicity.